Settling the Score

Season 1

by

Josh Hunter

© Josh Hunter, 2015

Originally published as the ebooks:
- *Settling the Score — Part 1: The Favor*
- *Settling the Score — Part 2: Blackmailed!*
- *Settling the Score — Part 3: The Cage*
- *Settling the Score — Part 4: Coach's Boy*

Part 1: The Favor

I was grabbing my books for history class when Wade Johnson came over and leaned against my locker. That could only mean trouble.

"Hey Kevin," he said, like we were friends.

"Wade."

I looked around for his minions. Wade always traveled with a posse of other football players. They were all like nineteen and twenty years old, and should have been in college by now. But in Texas, anybody who can throw a football gets held back a grade, so that they'll be bigger and stronger in their senior year.

Being able to pick on everybody else in the school is just an added bonus.

For once, though, Wade seemed to be alone. No sign of his goon squad.

He leaned in close to me.

"Look Kev, I need you to write an English paper for me."

So that was it.

"Forget it," I said.

Wade looked confused. He was used to people doing anything he asked.

"Awe, come on," he said, putting an arm around me like we were old buddies. "I'll owe you one."

"Fuck off, Wade. Get one of your football cronies to do it."

Wade rolled his eyes.

"I had Dwayne write my last paper. I got a fucking D- on it."

"Actually, Dwayne got the D-," I pointed out. "You just took the credit for it."

"Whatever. Now I've got to get an A- on this one or I get suspended from the team."

I laughed.

"Yeah right," I said. "Like the school would ever let *that* happen."

Wade shook his head.

"This new English teacher Pendergrass has it in for me. I think he'd really flunk me."

Wade had a point. I liked Mr. Pendergrass. He was probably the only teacher with the guts to fail a football player. Of course the school would fire him for it afterwards. This is Texas.

"And why would I want to help you?" I asked.

"Because . . . you know . . . . school pride," Wade said.

And then he turned on that thousand-watt smile. The smile that gets him anything he wants around this school. Well, that and the curly brown hair and the blue eyes and the body straight out of an Abercrombie & Fitch ad. And I guess the football thing, too. I could never understand why people get so excited about the fact that Wade can throw a stupid ball so far.

I looked right into that dazzling smile and told him to fuck off.

"Hey, don't be a fag!" Wade blurted out.

"That!" I said, slamming my locker closed. "That right there is why I don't want to help you. You've been calling me a fag since ninth grade."

"Jeez, sorry. I didn't know you were so sensitive."

I turned to go, but Wade grabbed me by the shoulder and pulled me back towards him.

"Okay, okay! I'll stop calling you a fag. But I need you to do this. You're smart. You could write a paper the way I would. Only, you know, good."

"Yeah, I could write 'good' if I wanted to."

"So do it!" Wade said. "If I don't play football this season, I'm screwed. No scholarship. No college. I'm dead meat."

I wanted to tell him to fuck off again. But I kind of enjoyed having Wade beg.

"Come on dude," he pleaded. "I'll do anything."

"*Anything?*" I asked.

"Yeah. Get you invited to parties. Introduce you to cheerleaders."

He lowered his voice to a whisper and leaned in close.

"I'll even tell my girlfriend to blow you."

Hm. Apparently, Wade's definition of "anything" was a little different than mine. But it would be fun to make him squirm a little.

"Okay," I said. "Come over to my house at eight. I'll help you write something that will pass muster with Pendergrass."

"Cool! You rock dude!"

He pointed his fingers at me like a pair of pistols, then turned and walked off.

I watched him go, thinking about all the crap that he'd pulled with me over the last few years.

It was time for Captain Cool to learn about payback.

* * *

Wade was late. It was 8:45 by the time he finally knocked on my front door.

"Hey," he said, without bothering to explain.

"Hi, Wade."

He stepped inside and looked around.

"Uh . . . where's your mom and dad?"

"Dad hasn't been around for years. My mom works nights. Did you bring your book?"

"Yeah," he reached into the pocket of his varsity jacket and pulled out a worn paperback.

"*Brave New World*," he said, handing it to me. "I picked it because there's supposed to be lots of sex and stuff."

Great. This wasn't going to be easy.

"Come on," I said. "My computer's back in my room."

He followed me down the hall.

"Could I get a beer?" he asked.

I turned and looked at him.

"Sure. My mom totally keeps the fridge stocked with beer for her underage son."

Wade's face brightened.

"Great! What kind?"

"That was sarcasm," I explained.

"Oh . . ." he said. "So no beer?"

"No beer."

We went back to my room and I sat down at my desk. Wade walked around, looking at the movie posters on my wall while I leafed through the book, reminding myself how it went.

"So how do we do this?" Wade asked.

"Well, for starters, tell me what you thought of the book."

"Uh . . ."

"And take your shirt off."

"Huh?"

Wade looked confused.

"I'm gonna help you with this, I should at least enjoy the view while I work."

A look of panic came into his eyes.

"Fuck! You really are a fag?"

"You've been calling me once since ninth grade."

"Yeah, but that was just . . . you know."

Wade was freaking out. For a moment I thought he might beat me up. Football player, gay boy. In Texas, nobody would even blink. But Wade seemed more confused than angry.

"You're really . . .?"

"Yeah. So you gonna lose that shirt now, or what?"

"Dude . . . I... I gotta go."

Wade headed for the bedroom door.

"Suit yourself," I said. "Paper is due tomorrow, right?"

Wade paused with his hand on the knob.

"I'm sure you can write an A paper on your own," I told him. "And even if you can't, it's only football. Right?"

Wade slowly turned back to me. He tried the smile again.

"Dude, you gotta help me with this," he begged.

"Dude, I don't even like you."

"Come on. I really need this!"

"So take off your shirt already."

He stood there, his face turning red.

"Come on," I told him. "You do it all the time in gym class."

"Yeah," he mumbled, "I guess."

He slowly took off his varsity jacket and put it on my bed. Then he finally pulled off his T-shirt. He stood there, nervously holding it.

I gave him a wolf whistle. The boy really did have one hell of a body.

His face turned a deeper shade of red.

"Stop looking at me that way."

"I'll look at you any damn way I want to. Now tell me what you remember from the book."

He sat down on my bed, still holding his shirt. Eventually, I got him to explain the book's theme and some of the basic plot.

"Hey, this isn't so hard," he said, warming up to the work.

"Yep," I agreed. "Now we just need to put it all in an outline."

"Okay."

"And you can take off your jeans now."

Wade laughed nervously.

"Yeah, right."

"I mean it. Strip down to your underwear."

"Awe, come on Kevin."

"What's the problem? Guys see you in your underwear in the locker room all the time."

"Yeah, but they don't look at me the way you do."

"And they're also not writing your fucking term paper for you. So lose the jeans."

Wade looked around nervously.

"You want this paper?" I asked.

Wade stood up and slowly fumbled with his belt buckle.

"You won't tell anybody about this?" he asked.

"Yeah, Wade. I'm gonna go around advertising the fact that I'm gay so that your football jerk friends will beat me to a pulp."

"This is so fucked up," Wade muttered.

He kicked off his shoes and unbuckled his belt. But then he seemed to lose his nerve.

"Now, Wade." I barked at him.

He unzipped his fly and slowly shucked off his jeans. Tighty whities. Figures.

He sat down on my bed, holding his hands in front of his crotch.

"Can we get on with this?" he asked.

"Sure thing, stud. First paragraph is going to be your thesis."

I walked him through the outline. Basic stuff. Thesis. Five supporting arguments. Conclusion. Crap I could do it in my sleep.

Wade started to relax again. He leaned back on my bed and let his legs spread apart. I could see the outline of his cock in his underwear.

Wade caught me staring.

"You really like looking at that?"

"Yep," I admitted. "Same way you like looking at pussy."

And I think Wade liked being looked at, too. Because the bulge in his underwear was getting bigger.

"How big are you?" I asked.

"I don't know," he said with a shrug.

"Bullshit," I said. "You know."

"Well, I'm not telling you."

He sat up and put his hands back in front of his crotch.

"Can I put my pants back on now?"

"Sure, if you want to finish this paper on your own."

"Fuck. Okay. What's next?"

"The rough draft."

"Okay. How do we do that?"

"First off, you can turn around. I want to look at your butt for a while."

"Jesus, Kevin!"

"After all the grief you've given me in the last three years, I'm entitled to a little payback."

Wade grumbled. But he couldn't see any way out of it. Reluctantly, he laid down on his stomach. The round curve of his ass showing nicely through the underwear.

"Just don't try to fucking touch me," he said.

"Yeah. 'Cause I could totally overpower you and have my way."

Wade laughed at that. He was four inches taller than me, with at least fifty pounds more muscle. It was kind of silly for him to be scared of me.

"You really get off on staring at my butt?" he asked.

"Hell yeah."

"Okay, just finish the damn paper."

I talked him through the next few paragraphs, but it was getting hard to concentrate. Looking at that tanned muscular body in my bed. Thinking about all the things I wanted to do to him. Trying to figure out just how far I could push Wade before he'd clobber me.

I pushed my chair back from my desk.

"Okay, I'm bored again," I said. "Pull down your underwear. I want to see some more of your ass."

"Really?"

Wade grumbled, but he'd lost enough arguments with me to know how this was going to play out. He slid his underwear down a couple of inches, showing me the crack of his butt.

"Happy?"

"Not yet," I said.

I walked over to the bed and slapped him hard on the ass.

"Ow! What the fuck was that for?"

"That was for *one* of the hundred thousand times you've called me a queer."

I grabbed the waistband of his underwear and started pulling it the rest of the way down. Wade grabbed my wrist.

'Hey! No way Kev!"

"You want this fucking paper?" I said, "I want to see your ass."

Wade tightened his grip on my wrist. I was gambling that the chance to play football would be more important than keeping some gay guy from seeing his butt. And I was right. Wade cursed and reluctantly let go of my wrist. I pulled his underwear off, sliding it down his legs and then tossing it on the floor.

"This is so fucked up," Wade muttered again.

"Yeah, well payback is a bitch."

I sat down at my desk and looked back at him. Wade Johnson naked in my bed. Who would have thought?

"Can we get this done?" Wade asked.

"Sure."

I went back to work on the paper. But not before I turned my webcam towards the bed and hit record. This was a view that I'd want to savor again.

I worked for another half hour, finishing up the draft, and glancing back at Wade every so often. He was getting restless.

"How late is it?" he asked, "Are you done?"

"A little after midnight. And no. I've got a rough draft. But I've still got to make it sound like you. Otherwise, Pendergrass will know that you outsourced it, and we'll both be dead."

"Okay."

I leaned back in my chair and stretched.

"You know, this is gonna take me a while. Roll over so that I can see the rest of you."

Wade frowned.

"Don't fuck with me, Kevin."

"It's a little late for that. I've put in hours of work on your fucking term paper, the least you can do is give me a show."

"Fuck off."

"Every guy on your stupid football team has already seen your dick in the shower."

"That's different."

"Yeah. I'll actually enjoy it."

"No."

"You want a term paper. I want to see your dick. What's it going to be?"

Wade looked mad enough to punch a hole in a wall, but he was stuck. He grabbed his varsity jacket and held it in front of his crotch as he rolled over to face me.

"Nope," I said, "No deal."

"Awe, come on!" Wade pleaded.

"Lose the jacket."

Wade's face burned a deep red. Slowly he pulled the jacket away and tossed it on the floor.

No wonder he'd been shy. The boy was semi-hard.

He put his hands in front of it.

"It's the way you look at me," he grumbled. "It makes me all nervous."

"Is that what you call it?"

I reached into my desk drawer and grabbed the little bottle of lotion I keep there. I tossed it to him.

"What's this?" he asked.

"Lube. As long as you're horny you may as well give me a show."

"Jeez, Kev."

"Just close your eyes and think of that hot cheerleader girlfriend of yours."

He looked at me, wondering if I really meant it.

"Or I could start deleting everything we've worked on tonight."

I turned back to my computer.

"Oh look. The last paragraph just got deleted. Now the next to the last paragraph. Now . . .."

"All right! All right!"

He popped open the bottle of lube, oiled up his dick, and went to work. He laid his head back on my pillow and closed his eyes. I watched him beat his meat for a couple of minutes, but he didn't seem to get any harder. I guess imagining the girlfriend wasn't doing it for him.

He opened his eyes and looked at me.

"Uh . . .. you got any porn?" he asked.

"Sure," I said.

I opened up some on my computer and then moved my chair out of the way so that he had a better view. Wade looked disgusted and turned his head away.

"I mean . . . you know . . . *straight* porn?"

"I can probably find some."

It took thirty seconds and a google search to dig up something that cranked his tractor. Blond girls with ridiculously big tits soaping each other up. Wade got rock hard and started working his dick faster and faster. But I noticed that he kept glancing away from the screen to look at me. I think he liked being watched. Feeling my eyes on his body. Some part of him was getting off on it.

I could hear him getting closer. His breathing getting faster. He looked away from the porn and stared right into my eyes. And then he came.

"Oh, Fuck!" he shouted, as he shot hot jizz out all over his stomach and chest. He grabbed his dick hard and threw his head back, his whole body shaking. "Fuck!"

I almost came just watching him.

After a few seconds, he managed to catch his breath. He raised his head and looked at me with those big blue eyes. We just stared at each other for a while without saying anything.

Finally, he looked down at the sticky mess on his chest.

"Uh, I'm kind of…."

I tossed him a box of Kleenex.

"Thanks."

He started wiping himself off.

"So, you're uh . . . happy now?" he asked. "You'll finish the paper?"

I grinned.

"Dude, I finished that paper an hour ago."

"What? Oh, you fucker."

Wade jumped to his feet. He grabbed his underwear off the floor and started pulling them on.

"Hey!" I barked at him. "Did I say you could get dressed?"

Wade paused.

"What now?"

"Nothing," I said. "I'm just fucking with you. You can put your clothes on."

Wade muttered a few curse words while he got dressed. By the time he was pulling on his varsity jacket I had "his" English paper printed and ready to go.

He held out his hand for it. But I had one more condition.

"And one more thing," I said. "You *never* call me a fag again."

Wade glared at me but grunted something that sounded like agreement. Then he snatched the paper and stormed out of the room. A few seconds later, I heard the front door slam.

I laughed and turned back to my computer to see how the video turned out. All in all, not a bad night.

* * *

The next few days were great. I'd see Wade around school, acting like nothing had happened. Joking with his idiot teammates. Making out with his cheerleader girlfriend between classes. But I knew. I knew what his naked body looked like under those clothes. The way his dick looked when it got hard. The way he moaned when he came.

And for the first time, I wasn't looking over my shoulder all day at school. Things had changed. I'd gotten a little something back from Wade, and I didn't have to take all the bullshit from him and his goon squad. Wade couldn't very well pick on me for being gay after he'd stripped down and jerked off for me.

My good mood lasted until Friday morning when I went to use the men's room. Wade and his posse were in there. Ordinarily, I would have turned around and left. Held it till the next class break. It just wasn't worth the hassle of dealing with those guys.

But I figured things were different now.

I walked up to the urinal next to Wade and started peeing. He didn't even glance at me.

"So how'd you do on your English paper?" I asked.

I knew I'd done A+ work for him, but I wanted to make sure that Pendegrass had thought so too.

"Uh . . . fine," Wade mumbled, staring straight ahead at the wall.

"Well, I guess that means you're still . . ."

I was about to congratulate him on keeping his place on the team, but I was stopped by a hard smack on the back of my head. It was one of Wade's football goons.

"Hey Wade, this faggot hassling you?"

I zipped my fly and turned around.

"Fuck off, asshole."

The goon looked surprised.

"What did you say to me, queer?"

"I told you to fuck off."

Another one of the goons walked over and shoved me back against the urinal.

"They letting queers in the men's room now? I think this guy was checking out your junk, Wade."

I almost laughed. I could watch Wade stroking his dick anytime I wanted on my laptop. It's not like I needed to watch him pee.

Then a third goon came over and shoved me as well. They're like a fucking pack of wolves. One of them smells weakness, and the others all join in. This was getting out of hand fast.

Good thing I had Wade to break this up. He owed me. I glanced at him, but he just stood there, his face turning red.

One of his thugs grabbed my shirt.

"Fucking queers in the men's room. Let's teach him a lesson."

The other two grabbed my arms. I struggled, but there were three of them and they were all built like ogres. They started dragging me towards one of the stalls.

"Wade!" I screamed, "Getting these fucking Neanderthals off me!"

But he stood there watching, not saying a thing.

The goons shoved me into one of the stalls and bent me over the toilet. One of them forced my face into the bowl. I fought like hell to get loose, but they were just too damn strong. They held my head underwater until my lungs burned. I thought I was going to pass out.

Finally, one of them grabbed my hair and pulled my head up.

"Say you're sorry, faggot!" he whispered in my ear.

"Fuck you!" I shouted, with all the breath I had left.

He slammed my head back into the toilet and held me under way too long. I kicked like crazy, thinking I was really going to drown. And then suddenly he let go and I was able to pull my face out.

Dripping wet and gasping for breath, I looked around. Behind the goons was Mr. Rhodes, the history teacher.

"You want to tell me what's going on here?" he asked.

The football players shrugged and grinned.

"Just having a little fun, sir."

I was struggling so hard to catch my breath that I couldn't say anything.

Mr. Rhodes looked us over.

"You're all late for third period. Get to class."

The goons all trooped out. Mr. Rhodes stared at me, sitting on the bathroom floor, sopping wet. I started to tell him what they'd done, but he turned and left.

Figures. The football players own this fucking school.

I skipped math class. I wasn't going to sit there with wet hair and let everyone know what had happened. And I needed time to think.

I found an isolated table in the library and got my laptop out. I watched the video of Wade again. I hadn't planned on using it for anything but my own amusement. But now this was war. And I was gonna use every weapon I had. It only took me a few minutes to get everything set up.

At lunch, I sat by myself. I watched Wade, at his table on the other side of the cafeteria. Surrounded by his football cronies. His girlfriend sitting in his lap, feeding him french fries. He was smiling, like he was the king of the fucking world.

I got out my phone and sent him the text.

Across the room, I saw Wade laughing at something his girlfriend had said. He reached into his pocket to answer his phone. He looked at the screen . . . and his expression froze. He went white as a ghost. And then he quickly shoved the phone back into his pocket before anyone could see.

He looked around the lunch room in a panic. And then finally his gaze stopped on me. I smiled and waved. And then Wade's big blue eyes went wide with fear.

His girlfriend leaned in to say something. Wade forced a smile and tried to act causal. But he was freaking out. I watched him squirm his way through the rest of lunch.

I got his first text as I was heading into chemistry.

"What do you want?"

I didn't respond. I figured Wade could stew for a while. Wondering what I was going to do next. Who else I was going to show that pic to?

He kept texting me all through the next few classes.

"Dude, you can't show that to anyone."

"Plz don't show that to anyone."

"You haven't shown it to anyone, have you?"

I let him simmer until a few minutes before last period. Then I finally sent a reply.

"The roof. Now. Or the whole school sees it."

I headed to the back of the school. There's an old tree that you can climb to get up on the roof. Most everybody knows about it. Sometimes kids go up there to smoke or make out. But today I had it to myself.

Wade climbed up a few minutes later. He looked around, nervous that he might be seen with me.

"Dude, why did you take that picture?" he asked.

"It's not a picture," I told him. "It's video. Have a look."

I held up my phone. There on the screen was Wade, crying out as cum shot all over his stomach. And then turning to me and asking if that's what I'd wanted.

Wade looked like he was going to have a heart attack. He tried to grab my phone, but I jerked it back out of his reach.

"That's not the only copy, Einstein. I've already uploaded it to the web."

Wade froze.

"You mean everyone can see that?"

"Not yet. It's password protected. For now."

Wade looked me over, trying to figure out how much trouble he was in.

"What do you want?" he asked.

That was the question.

"Maybe I just want to watch what happens when the rest of the football team sees this. What do you think they'll do when they find out you've been doing gay sex shows to pass English?"

Wade swallowed hard.

"Dude, you can't."

"Or it might be fun to watch what your girlfriend does when she finds out that you've been beating off for a gay guy."

"No, please don't . . ."

"Or all those college recruiters. What do you think they'll say when they see it?"

Wade looked like he was about to cry.

"Please," he begged, "You can't do this."

"You should have thought of that before you let your goons shove my head in the toilet."

"It's not the same!" Wade protested. "So your hair got a little wet. What's the big deal?"

I stared at him.

"*What's the big deal?*" I repeated back.

Wade looked at me blankly.

And then I realized that he really didn't get it. He'd always been the golden boy that everyone kisses up to. He'd never been on the receiving end of his friends' "jokes". He'd never been bullied, or scared, or not in control.

It was time he got a fucking education.

"Look, I'm sorry," Wade said. "Is that what you want to hear?"

"We're way past that," I told him.

He stood there, shaking, on the verge of tears.

"Please," he begged. "I'll do anything."

I turned to go.

"My house," I told him, as I walked away. "Ten pm tonight."

* * *

There was a knock on the door at 11:15. I opened it to find Wade standing on the front porch, looking around nervously.

"You're late," I told him.

"Whatever. Let me in before someone sees me here."

Wade stepped into the hallway and I closed the door behind him. He reached into his varsity jacket and pulled out a wad of bills and a small plastic bag.

"I've got a couple hundred dollars here. And this is all the weed I could get my hands on."

Nice try. He wasn't getting off that easy.

"I don't want your money or your fucking weed," I told him.

And then I thought better of it.

"No, wait," I said. "Give me the money. But I'll give you a chance to earn it back."

Wade handed over the bills and stuffed the weed back in his pocket.

"So we're good now?" he asked hopefully.

"Not by a long shot. This way."

I led him into the den. I had some dance music playing, and I'd set up a little disco lights machine that I'd gotten at the mall. It was tacky, but it set the mood.

"Uh . . . what's all this?" Wade asked.

I sat down on the couch.

"This is where you start earning my forgiveness," I told him. "I thought we'd start with a strip show."

Wade laughed nervously.

"I just gave you two hundred bucks, Kev. We're even. I'm not playing any more of your stupid games."

I shrugged.

"Well, if you don't feel like dancing, I guess we can watch TV instead."

I picked up the remote. The video of Wade jerking off came to life on the screen, and the room filled with the sound of him getting ready to cum.

"Oh . . . fuck . . . oh!"

Wade grimaced and turned away from the TV.

"Sorry," I shouted over his recorded moans, "I forgot how loud you get towards the end there."

I hit the mute button.

Wade glared at me.

"You can't show that to anyone."

"Oh yes I can," I corrected him. "I've already uploaded it to X-tube. It's scheduled to go live at midnight."

Wade glanced at the clock, and a look of panic crossed his face.

"It's called *Quarterback Sex Show,*" I told him, "and I tagged it with your real name. So it will turn up every time someone googles you. How long do you think it will take before someone at school finds it and starts passing it around?"

Wade clenched his fists and took a step toward me.

"I'm gonna beat your queer ass into the ground for this."

I looked him square in the eye.

"Go ahead. And then who's gonna stop that video from going out?"

Wade froze in his tracks.

"You can stop it?"

I shrugged.

"Sure. If I wanted to."

Wade stood there, clenching and unclenching his fists. Angry, and frustrated, but mostly scared. His whole world was about to unravel.

"So stop it," he pleaded.

"Here's your problem, Wade: I don't like you. You've been a total dick to me since the day we met. And today you let your goons try to drown me in a toilet. So I'm gonna enjoy watching you go down."

Wade's face turned red, and tears started welling up in his eyes. He looked like he was either gonna punch me or cry. Or maybe both. He took another look at his video, playing silently on the TV.

"I'm sorry!" he blurted out. "Okay? What am I supposed to do?"

"In your shoes? I'd find a way to make me like you. And I'd try *real* hard. You've got thirty-five minutes to make me forget three years of your fucking abuse."

Wade stood there, trying to think of some way out of this. But thinking had never been Wade's strong suit.

"Make that thirty-four minutes," I said, pointing to the clock.

Wade bit his lip. He stared at the floor for a few seconds. And then he slowly took off his varsity jacket.

"Woo-hoo!" I cheered. "Looks like we've got a new performer in the champagne room."

Wade just kept staring at the floor.

"You're not filming me this time, are you?"

"My computer's in my bedroom," I told him. Which was technically true. Of course, with wi-fi enabled cameras it doesn't matter where my computer is. But Wade didn't need to know that.

He started unbuttoning his shirt, revealing his smooth tanned chest.

I shook my head.

"Wow, you suck at this," I told him.

Wade looked up at me, confused.

"I thought . . . this is what you want, right?"

"I want a *show*. If you want to me forget all the bullshit you've pulled with me, you're gonna have to try harder than that."

I turned up the volume on the music. Wade awkwardly shifted his weight from foot to foot.

I groaned.

"God, even you can't be this bad a dancer."

"Fuck off, Kev. It's not like I've done this before."

"Bullshit. I've seen the way you dance with your girlfriend. Try that."

Wade forced himself to loosen up. Moving his hips. Making crazy gestures with his arms. He wasn't gonna win any dance contests, but at least he was trying.

He slowly popped another button on his shirt, and then looked over to me for approval.

"Yeah, that's better."

Wade slowly worked his way out of the shirt. Showing off his chest, his tight abs, his muscular shoulders. He kept glancing over at me like he wanted to make sure I was paying attention. And he was a hell of a sexy guy. Terrible dancing aside, he could probably have a career with Chippendales.

He finally slid the shirt off altogether and threw it on the floor.

I held up one of the twenties from his roll of bills.

"Come over here, sweet cheeks."

Wade awkwardly danced over to the couch. I reached up and felt his chest. Ran my hand over the warm skin of his stomach. He trembled a little but didn't stop me.

"Nice body," I told him, tucking the bill into his jeans. "Let's see some more of it."

Wade reached for his belt buckle and then lost his nerve. He froze like that.

"Twenty minutes till midnight," I reminded him.

Wade looked back at the TV, where his video had looped back to the beginning. He swallowed hard and unbuckled his belt. I could see his hands shaking as he unbuttoned the fly of his jeans. And then he slowly unzipped them.

He was so hard he was practically popping out of his tighty whities.

"I think you like this job," I told him, as I stuffed another twenty into the waistband of his underwear.

"It's just the way you look at me," he mumbled. "It fucks with my head."

Wade kicked off his shoes, and slowly shucked off his jeans. He stood there in front of me, the bulge in his underwear only a few inches from my face.

"Turn around," I told him.

Wade did as he was told. He looked back over his shoulder at me. And then he pulled his underwear down to show me his smooth round ass.

"Is that what you wanted to see?"

I guess the grin on my face was enough of an answer. He pulled off his underwear and threw them aside. And then he slowly turned around. He just stood there, his hard cock bobbing in front of my face. He looked down at me with those big blue eyes.

"Okay, you got your strip show, Kev. Now cancel the video."

"Nah," I said, holding up his money. "I've still got a wad of bills here. And I want a lap dance."

Wade glanced at the clock.

"Kev, there's only ten minutes left."

"Then you'd better give me one hell of a lap dance."

I grabbed his waist and pulled him down towards me. He knelt on the couch, straddling me, his naked body pressing against my clothes. I could feel him trembling.

"Nine minutes," I reminded him. "And you still haven't earned my forgiveness."

Wade took the hint. He started moving his hips, grinding his ass against my jeans, his cock slapping against my stomach.

"Yeah, that's it."

I ran my hands over his chest, his shoulders, over every inch of his perfect body. I could see his cock getting harder. I pulled him close, and put my mouth on one of his nipples. He let out a little whimper, and I could feel it getting hard under my tongue.

"Is this what you wanted, Kev?" he whispered, his breath hot in my ear. "Are we good now?"

I slid a hand between his legs and let my fingers brush against his nuts. He let out a little gasp. And then I wrapped my hand around his dick.

His hand shot down and grabbed my wrist.

"No, don't do that . . ." he pleaded.

But I could feel his dick getting bigger and harder in my hand. A warm drop of precum ran down my fingers, and his grip on my wrist weakened.

I started stroking his cock. I could feel his whole body shaking. I only got a couple good pumps in before he let out a moan and buried his face in my neck. And then all of a sudden he was shooting hot jizz all over my shirt.

"Fuck . . .. oh . . . fuck!"

He collapsed on top of me, panting. He lay there for a few seconds, catching his breath. And then he remembered the time.

He raised his head and looked back at the clock.

"Shit, there's only five minutes left."

He rolled off me and fell back onto the couch.

"Okay, Kev. You got your show. Now make that video go away."

I sat there, feeling his warm cum soaking through my shirt.

"No," I said. "We're still not even."

"What? But I've done everything you wanted!"

"Not *everything*," I told him, as I undid the buckle on my belt.

I unzipped my fly and whipped out my cock. Wade's eyes went wide. He had fifty-pound pounds of muscle on me. But I had it all over him in the dick department.

"We're not even until we *both* get off," I told him.

Wade stared at my cock.

"Five minutes," I reminded him.

"I . . . I can't."

"Then our school is about to have its first porn star."

I put a hand on the back of his neck and guided his face down towards my crotch.

"I'm not a fag," Wade protested.

"And I don't care."

I felt his hot breath on the head of my cock. And then a tentative touch of his tongue, like he was trying to see what it tasted like. And then the head slid past his lips and I was getting my first blow job.

It was even better than I'd imagined. The feel of his hot wet mouth on my dick. The sight of his head bobbing up and down, as he struggled to get me off before his time ran out.

I fought to keep myself from cumming. It felt so good that I didn't want him to stop. But then Wade looked up at me with those big blue eyes. His lips wrapped tight around my dick. And I thought about all the times he called *me* a cocksucker.

And suddenly I was shooting my load in his mouth. Wade grimaced and spat out my dick, but the second blast caught him in the face. Then my cock slapped down against my stomach, pumping out the rest of its load onto my shirt. My cum mingling with his.

Wade spat into his hand and tried to wipe the cum off his face. He stared up at me with pleading eyes. I reached down and ran my fingers through his curly brown hair.

"*Now* we're even," I told him.

I pulled out my phone to cancel the video's release. We had a whole thirty seconds to spare.

Part 2: Blackmailed!

The next day Wade was back to acting like the king of high school. I watched him holding court during lunch. Joking around with the football players, making out with his cheerleader girlfriend. The golden boy jock who rules this place.

But every so often he'd glance over in my direction. We'd make eye contact for a few seconds, and then his face would turn all red and he'd look away.

Yeah, Wade. Go ahead and act like nothing has changed. But we both know that you had your lips wrapped around my dick last night.

I couldn't help but grin. Unfortunately, his girlfriend caught me staring. She giggled and pointed at me.

"Hey, Wade! I think someone's got a crush on you."

Wade laughed nervously and tried to play it cool.

"Fags," he said with a shrug. "What you gonna do?"

That was all the encouragement that his minions needed. A football player named Logan jumped up and came over to my table.

"Yeah, fag. Is that what you want? You hoping to suck Wade's dick?"

There was a ripple of laughter, and I suddenly realized that the whole lunch room was looking at me. And now it was my face that was turning red.

Logan was shorter than Wade, but even more muscled, with arms like fucking sledgehammers. I'm guessing steroids were involved. He kept his blond hair in a short crew cut. He looked like some Army recruiter's wet dream.

Logan leaned over the table and got right in my face.

"Didn't you hear me faggot? I asked if you wanted to suck Wade's dick?"

The laughter got louder. Logan looked back over his shoulder at Wade.

"Hey, Wade! What do you think we should do with..."

Logan stopped talking when my fist smashed into his face.

I didn't even know that I was going to do it. I was just so sick of Wade and Logan and their whole fucking clique.

Logan stumbled backward a few steps, and the whole lunch room went silent. He looked around, surprised. Like he couldn't understand what had just happened. And then the other football players stood up.

I didn't care. I leapt out of my chair.

"You want a piece of me assholes?" I screamed. "Come and get it!"

I don't know what I was thinking. Any one of those guys could have beaten me to a pulp. They're twice my size, and it's not like I even know how to fight. But something had snapped inside me, and I wasn't going to take it anymore.

"Parker!" someone yelled in my ear. "What the hell is going on here?"

I turned and saw Mr. Pendergrass standing next to me.

"Uh..."

"Principal's office. Now!" he shouted.

Well, getting busted by a teacher was a heck of a lot better than getting massacred by the football team. I followed Pendergrass out of the lunchroom. On the walk to the Principal's office he tried to make me see the error of my ways.

"You can't just go around hitting people," he said. "That's not going to solve anything."

"Oh yeah? And where were you when those guys were trying to drown me in a toilet yesterday?"

That seemed to shut him up.

As for the Principal, he was kind of in a bind over what to do with me. On the one hand, I'd struck a football player-- which in West Texas is pretty much like spitting on the Bible or something. On the other hand, the Principal seemed kind of amused that a geek like me had gotten in a lick on one of the jocks and lived to tell about it.

In the end, the Principal sent me home with a one-day suspension. He also tried to call my mom, but luckily she works nights and wouldn't be awake for another hour or so. I'd have to figure out what to tell her when I got home.

But in the meantime, I was going to have a word with Wade. On my way out of the Principal's office, I sent him a text.

"Roof. Now. Or the whole school sees your jackoff video."

I got there first. Luckily no one else was around. This soon after lunch, I guess nobody needed a smoke break. Wade climbed up a few minutes later.

"I can't stay long," he said. "I'm cutting history."

"I'm sure it's not the first time."

He looked around nervously, making sure we were alone.

"Dude, why did you have to go ballistic on Logan like that?"

"*Dude*, why did your fucking minion have to get up in my face like that?"

Wade shook his head.

"This is so fucked up. My whole posse is gonna be gunning for you now."

"So call 'em off."

"I can't do that!" Wade said. "You're a fag."

I smacked him on the side of the head.

"Hey! You don't get to call me that anymore. Remember?"

"Well, you are!" Wade protested. "And if we're suddenly best buddies, everyone will think that I'm one, too. You're just gonna have to watch out for yourself."

"Fuck that," I said. "Maybe your buddies should start watching out for *me*."

Wade laughed.

"You are a cocky son of a bitch," he said. "I'll give you that."

"Yeah. And in case you've forgotten, I'm also the son of a bitch who can make you a porn star."

Wade stopped laughing.

"You can't do that," he said. "We're even."

"We *were* even," I corrected him. "That was before you sicked Logan on me at lunch."

"That wasn't my fault!"

"Bullshit. Logan is your little bitch. The only reason he came after me is because you called me a faggot."

"Yeah, but I didn't mean for him to . . ."

"You didn't?"

Wade stood there silently for a few seconds. Logical thinking isn't his strong suit.

"What are you gonna do, Kev?"

"I don't know. Maybe I should post your jack-off video for everybody to see. I'll bet they'd be so busy ripping you a new one that they'd forget all about me."

Wade turned white.

"You wouldn't do that," he said.

I looked him right in the eye.

"Give me one good reason not to."

Wade swallowed hard.

"Uh... I could... you know... blow you again?"

I raised an eyebrow.

Wade looked around, then stepped closer to me. He put his arm around my shoulder, like we were buddies or something.

"Come on, Kev. You liked what I did. One more time and we'll be even, right?"

His leg brushed against mine. It was hard for me to think with Wade this close. His face just a few inches from mine. I knew I should be pissed at him, but damn that boy is sexy.

"Okay," I whispered, and started unbuckling my belt.

"Jeez! Not here!" Wade said.

"You gonna make this right or not?" I asked.

"Yeah... but, what if someone comes along?"

I took out my cock, already semi-hard. Wade looked around nervously.

"You'd rather the whole school sees your sex tape?" I asked.

I put a hand on Wade's shoulder and pushed him down on his knees. He knelt there, so close that I could feel his breath on my cock.

"Come on," I told him. "The longer it takes, the more chance we get caught."

Wade hesitated for a few seconds. And then he opened his mouth and slid my cock into it.

Fuck. It was even better than the first time. Wade's warm wet mouth on the head of my dick. His lips wrapped tight around the shaft. His big blue eyes looking up at me while he struggled to get me off as quickly as he could. It almost made it worth all the bullshit he'd just put me through.

And honestly, I didn't care if someone did see us. Sure, Wade's social life would implode. But it's not like mine could get any worse. Everyone already figured I was gay. Being the gay guy who got caught receiving a blowjob from the quarterback would probably be a step up in the world.

I was starting to relax and get into it when there was a loud noise right behind me. Wade jumped to his feet, while I tried to stuff my rock-hard cock back into my pants.

I saw the panicked look on Wade's face, and then I saw him relax.

"It's okay," he said. "It's just a tree branch hitting the wall."

I had to admit that I was relieved, too. Maybe I wasn't quite ready to be the talk of the school yet.

I looked down at the awkward bulge in my jeans.

"You gonna finish what you started?" I asked.

Wade shook his head.

"It's too damn risky here. Let me come over to your house tonight."

"I don't know," I said. "Tonight's a long way off. And I'm horny now."

I reached into my jeans and started to pull my dick back out.

"Just cool your fucking jets!" Wade pleaded. "I'll come over tonight. I'll do anything you want, okay?"

That's what I wanted to hear.

"Okay," I told him. "8 pm. Don't be late."

* * *

Mom hit the roof when she found out that I'd been suspended from school for fighting. I tried to explain that it wasn't my fault, that Logan had started it. But she was in full irrational "mom mode", and there was no reasoning with her. In the end, she told me that I was "grounded", which is some sort of prehistoric punishment from back when she was a kid. I mean, she works all night. So short of an ankle bracelet I don't know how she planned on keeping me from leaving the house. And I don't have a car, so where the hell would I go, anyway?

Well, there was no point arguing with her. I played the "good boy" and got out my books to study. But I was way too distracted for homework. I kept thinking about Wade, and all the fun I was going to have with him in a few hours. I got so horny that I had to keep a book in my lap so that mom wouldn't see my boner. By the time she finally left for work at 7:30, I was so worked up that I thought I would explode.

With mom out of the house, I waited for Wade. But eight o'clock came and went, and Wade didn't turn up. Then 8:30. Then 9 pm. By 9:30 I was past horny and into frustrated and pissed off.

Finally, at 9:45 someone rang the doorbell. I opened the door and Wade was standing there. His eyes on the ground, his hands shoved in the pockets of his varsity jacket.

"You're late," I told him. "Again."

"Whatever," he mumbled.

He stepped inside and looked around nervously.

"My mom's at work," I told him.

"Yeah... okay."

There was a tremor in his voice, and he sounded scared. The last time he'd come over, he'd figured he could buy his way out with cash and weed. This time, he knew exactly what he was here to do.

His eyes landed on my jeans, and the shape of my hard cock pressing against the denim. That's the problem with being big. It's really obvious when I get excited.

Wade swallowed.

"So.... uh.... how do you want to do this?"

"Strip naked," I told him.

Wade gave an awkward little chuckle, like he didn't think I was serious.

"Uh... right here?"

"Now," I told him. "I've been waiting long enough."

Wade's hands were trembling as he took them out of his pockets. He pulled off his varsity jacket and held it awkwardly.

"Where should I...?"

"Throw it on the fucking floor," I told him.

Wade let go of the jacket. He looked at me, and then unbuttoned his shirt. My hard cock twitched as Wade's tanned chest came into view, then his tight abs. That boy really was too sexy for words.

Wade looked up, like was waiting for my approval or something.

"Keep going," I told him.

Wade dropped his shirt on the floor, and then bent over to take off his shoes and socks. Then he stood back up and fumbled clumsily with his belt. I watched him struggle with the buckle for a few seconds before he finally got it. He stared at the floor as he unzipped his fly, and slowly shucked off his jeans. And then he just stood there, shaking a little, the bulge in his tighty whities getting bigger.

"I said, 'naked', Wade."

Wade bit his lip. He hesitated for a moment, and then pulled off his underwear. His erect cock popped out, bobbing in the air in front of him like a fishing pole.

I let him stand there for a while, just so I could look at him. He was so fucking beautiful it made my dick ache.

But he'd also been making me wait all night.

"This way," I said, leading him into the kitchen.

I motioned for him to stand in front of the table and then told him to bend over. Wade looked confused.

"Just do it," I barked.

Wade leaned over and put his hands on the table.

"Like this?" he asked.

"No, lower," I told him.

I put a hand on the back of his neck and shoved his face down on the table.

"Now stay there."

I took a step back. And then I slapped his ass, hard.

"Ow!" Wade shouted.

He stood up and rubbed his butt.

"What the hell, Kev?"

"That was for making me wait."

Wade started to say something, but I cut him off.

"And I didn't say you could stand up."

Wade looked at me uncertainly. Then he turned around and slowly bent over the table again.

I slapped his ass, so hard it made my hand sting. Wade grimaced in pain.

"And that one's for calling me a fag."

I slapped him again, as hard as I could. Wade groaned and gripped the sides of the table.

"And that's for all the grief I'm getting from Logan and your fucking goon squad."

And then I really let him have it. Smacking him over and over, until his ass was bright red. Wade clenched his teeth, trying to take it in silence. But he couldn't. After every blow, a short little grunt of pain would get past his lips. And no wonder. If his ass was half as sore as my hand, he was in a world of hurt.

"I'm sorry," he finally blurted out. "Okay? It won't happen again."

"Damn right," I said.

I hit him one more time for good measure. And then I stepped back and took a few seconds to catch my breath. My arm was tired. I shook my hand, trying to get the feeling back in my fingers. Wade stayed in the position, waiting for whatever came next.

I walked back over to him. Wade tensed up, expecting another spanking. But I just ran a hand over his ass, all red and hot from his punishment. And then I stepped in closer, grinding the bulge in my jeans against his naked butt.

Wade lifted his head off the table and looked back at me.

"What are you doing, Kev?"

"Just stay there."

I unzipped my fly and pulled out my hard dick. I slapped it against his ass a couple of times.

"Uh... Kev... you're not...."

"Shut up, Wade. You said you'd do *anything* to make this right. Remember?"

I spit in my hand and slicked up my dick. And then I grabbed the shaft and guided it between Wade's legs. I pressed the slippery head of my cock up against his tight little asshole and started to push.

Wade jerked up so fast that it knocked me off my feet. I stumbled backward, and landed hard on the kitchen floor. I tried to get up, but Wade tackled me. He grabbed me by the throat and pinned me down.

"Get this straight, faggot! I am not like you!" he shouted, his face only a few inches from mine. "And I am *never* gonna take it up the ass, no matter what."

He held me down like that, his naked body heavy on top of me. His breath hot on my face. A crazy, desperate look in his eyes. And his raging hard-on rubbing against my stomach.

I reached down between us to grab it. Wade inhaled sharply, and I felt his dick jump in my hand.

Wade's grip on my throat relaxed. I stroked his cock a few times, and felt his hot precum trickling down my fingers. He stared into my eyes, looking frightened.

I grabbed my own cock and rubbed it against his. Wade bit his lip and let out a little whimper. I jerked us off together, our slick dicks sliding against each other.

Wade moaned softly. I wrapped my free arm around him, my hand on his back, holding him close. I could feel him trembling.

"Oh, fuck!" he moaned.

And then all of a sudden Wade was cumming. I felt his hot jizz erupt all over the head of my cock, and that was enough to set me off, too. I clenched my teeth and threw my head back as my own dick cut loose in response.

I don't know if Guinness keeps track of these things, but Wade's orgasm must have been one for the record books. He came so hard that his whole body shook, as load after load of his hot jizz splashed over my dick.

"Fuck," he kept moaning, "Of fuck!"

And then he finally finished and collapsed on top of me, panting.

We lay there for a while, too tired to move, trying to catch our breath. Wade's naked body pressing down on me. Our warm cum soaking through my t-shirt.

After a minute or so, Wade lifted his head. He looked down at me with those bright blue eyes for a while. He seemed like he wanted to say something.

But then he just shook his head and rolled off me.

"I gotta go," he said, standing up.

"Yeah," I agreed. "We're done."

For now.

* * *

The next morning I woke up and started getting ready for school. And then I remembered that I was suspended for the day. And "grounded". Ugh.

Well, at least I had a few hours to myself before mom woke up. I picked up my clothes and started a load of laundry. No point in letting mom wonder how I'd managed to get cum stains all over my shirt. And besides, it gave me some time to think about Wade.

The whole situation was completely fucked up. I hadn't planned on pushing things this far. But Wade was like some kind of drug. The more I got of him, the more I wanted. I couldn't stop myself.

And why should I even try? Wade and his football goons have been making my life miserable for years. Why shouldn't I turn the tables on him now that I had the chance? Make Wade choke on the word "fag" while he sucks my dick. Make him spread his legs and give up his tight little ass. And then look him in the eye and say "I won, motherfucker."

And the fact that Wade swears that he'll never "take it up the butt"? That's just gonna make it all the sweeter. The question was how to do it. How to break him. How to get Wade to the point that he'd do *anything* I wanted.

For once, Google let me down. A search for "How to fuck a straight boy" turned up a bunch of porn videos but little practical advice. I tried all kinds of variations, but the only thing I could find were a few articles on obedience training for dogs.

Well, I figured that Wade isn't much smarter than a cocker spaniel, so I gave the obedience training articles a read. It looked like some of the same rules might apply. I'd already stumbled across "negative feedback": Wade pisses me off, his ass takes a whipping. And as for "positive feedback"... well, I wasn't having any trouble making Wade cum.

The problem was that I had a lot of competition in that department. Wade could fuck his girlfriend anytime he wanted... or pretty much any other girl in school for that matter. So Wade would never need me as badly as I needed him. It's like trying to train a puppy when everyone else keeps tossing it treats.

I needed some way to control Wade's sex life. To make it so that I was the only one who could get him off. Then I would really have him by the balls.

This time, Google was a bit more helpful. And luckily, Amazon has overnight shipping. Wade was in for a big surprise.

* * *

At school the next day, everyone was staring at me and whispering. I wasn't sure why, but then I caught sight of Logan. He had a huge black shiner from where I'd punched him in the eye on Wednesday.

As soon as he saw me, he came storming down the hall like a charging bull. I turned to run, but another football player was right behind me. A wall of muscle named Tyler. He had dark hair and the sort of chest you normally see in comic books. In the right costume, he could have passed for Superman.

If Superman was a complete asshole.

Tyler shoved me into the lockers, which gave Logan enough time to catch me. He grabbed me by the shirt.

"You are so fucking dead, *faggot*."

The hallway went silent, as everyone turned to watch me get my beatdown. But then I saw Mr. Pendergrass come out of his classroom.

"Is there a problem here?" he asked, walking over.

"No, sir. No problem," Logan said.

"Then maybe you should all get to your next class."

Logan reluctantly let go of my shirt.

"We'll settle this later," he whispered.

Logan and Tyler walked off together. As they got to the end of the hall, Logan looked back at me and drew his finger across his throat. I hurried off to history.

After class, I discovered that I'd picked up a tail. Logan and Tyler, following me down the hall. Probably hoping to corner me in the bathroom between classes. Well, I could hold it for a few hours if had to.

As for Wade, I didn't see him again until lunch. He and his posse were at their usual table. Logan and Tyler chewed their sandwiches and glared at me, while Wade and his girlfriend made out. Well, "made out" is a bit of an understatement. The two of them were going at it so hot and heavy that a teacher finally went over and broke it up. Apparently, there are limits to what even Wade can get away with at this school.

After lunch, Logan and Tyler followed me down the hall again. But I got lucky and saw Mr. Pendergrass going into the men's room. I scurried in after him, figuring that I'd better grab a chance to piss while it was safe. Logan and Tyler followed me in, but then they saw Pendergrass standing at the urinal next to mine. They stood there awkwardly for a few seconds, and then finally turned around and left.

Pendergrass looked over at me.

"You're going to have to figure out some way to deal with that. I can't be around all the time."

"Tell me something I don't know," I said, zipping my fly.

I got to Chemistry class and fired off a text to Wade.

"Get your fucking goons off my case."

His answer was waiting for me after class.

"Can't. Whole school saw you layout Logan. Everyone ribbing him about losing a fight to a fag. He's pissed."

Fucking football players.

"Then you're gonna have to answer for Logan's bullshit," I texted back. "My house, 8 pm."

Wade took a couple minutes to respond.

"I can't. I have a date with Brittany tonight."

Wade. He acted like this was a social call.

"You can fuck your girlfriend when I'm done with you," I texted back.

And then I sent him a pic from his jerk-off video, just to remind him who's boss.

I made it through history and managed to avoid any run-ins with the goon squad for the rest of the school day. Logan and Tyler kept following me around between classes, but I wasn't about to go anyplace where they could jump me without a teacher intervening.

They did almost get me after school, though. I was walking across the parking lot when I spotted the two of them behind me. Luckily, they stand out in a crowd. I wasn't about to let the two of them corner me on my walk home, so I turned around and circled back into school. I figured it was time to make use of a little something that the football players have probably never heard of.

Study hall.

I grabbed a desk right in front of Mrs. Simmons and got out my homework. Logan and Tyler stuck their heads in the door a few times, looking pissed off. But after ten minutes they finally gave up and went to football practice.

Pendergrass was right. I was going to have to figure out some way to handle those two.

Anyway, with tweedle-dee and tweedle-dum out of the way, I jogged home. I was happy to see that the boxes from Amazon had arrived. It's a good thing mom doesn't open my mail, or she would have gotten one hell of a surprise this time.

The rest of the afternoon seemed to go by in slow motion. I tried to get some schoolwork done, but all I could think about was Wade.

Mom chattered away during dinner, talking about all the crap that was happening with her job at the hospital. At least she's given up asking me about girls and school. And then she finally left for work at 7:30.

I got everything set up, and then paced around, waiting for Wade. Eight pm came, but Wade didn't. 8:10. 8:20. I was beginning to wonder if he was going to show. Did he think I was bluffing about the video?

Finally, at nine o'clock the doorbell rang. I opened the door and Wade came in, a sullen look on his face.

"You know the drill," I told him. "Strip down."

"This isn't fair," Wade muttered, but he did as he was told. Peeling off his jacket, his shirt, his jeans. Finally, he shucked off his underwear, and stood there naked, staring at the floor.

I still can't get over how beautiful he is. Like Michelangelo's statue of David. Only better. That statue doesn't have a raging boner.

"On your knees," I told him.

Wade knelt down. I stood in front of him and ran my fingers through his curly brown hair. He looked up at me.

"You can't keep making me do this, Kev."

"Oh yes I can," I corrected him. "Now stay."

Time to see if that obedience training manual knew what it was talking about. I went to my room and returned with Wade's new collar.

"What the hell is that for?" Wade asked.

"To remind you of your fucking place," I told him, as I buckled the thick leather strap around his neck.

Wade shot me a disgusted look.

"You're weird," he mumbled.

I grabbed him by the collar and pulled him to his feet.

"This way, boy."

I marched him into the kitchen and over to the table.

"No!," Wade protested, "Not this again. I didn't do anything!"

"Yeah, " I agreed, "You didn't tell Logan and Tyler to back off and leave me alone. So bend over."

Wade hesitated.

"I'm not gonna take it in the ass," he said. "You know that, right?"

"Yeah, I heard. Now bend over the fucking table."

Wade reluctantly assumed the position. I went over to the counter and came back with my second new toy. A hardwood paddle.

The first blow landed on his ass with a loud crack. Wade let out a howl of pain and stood up.

"What the fuck!" he shouted, feeling his backside.

"Take your punishment like a man," I told him.

Wade looked at the paddle, and then shook his head.

"No way. That thing hurts too much."

"You'd rather be the school's new porn star?" I asked him.

Wade frowned and grudgingly turned back around. He slowly bent over the table.

I landed another hard blow on his ass. Wade clenched his teeth, trying not to cry out.

"That's for making me wait. *Again*."

I hit him even harder. This time Wade couldn't help it. He yelped in pain.

"I'm sorry," blurted out.

"Is it going to happen again?" I asked.

"No!"

I smacked his butt again. Wade made a little whimpering sound and buried his face against the table.

"So when I tell you to be somewhere, you'll be there?"

"Yes sir!"

I liked the way he said, "sir". It made my dick tingle.

I hit him again, and Wade cried out in pain.

"And that's for starting all this bullshit with Logan."

"I'm sorry!"

"And that's for not stopping it."

I smacked him again and again. Ticking off every fucking thing that Wade had ever done to piss me off. Till his ass was cherry red and Wade was blubbering like a baby.

"I'm sorry Kev," Wade sobbed, "I'm so sorry!"

I pulled back the paddle for another swing, and held it there for a few seconds. Letting Wade wonder if he had another one coming. And then I slowly put the paddle down on the table next to him. Wade let out a final sob and shuddered with relief.

I sat down in one of the kitchen chairs and unzipped my jeans.

"Okay, boy. Show me how sorry you are."

Wade stood up and wiped the tears off his face. He watched, as I pulled out my dick. He stared at it for a few seconds, sniffling. And then he knelt down in front of me and went to work.

The feel of his tongue on my cock was electric. And Wade was getting better with practice. He licked the head, then wrapped his lips tight around the shaft. He tried different things, looking up to see what I liked, what was pleasing me. After that paddling, sucking my dick must have seemed like a relief, an easy way to get back in my good graces. Which was the whole idea.

"Good boy," I told him, as he tried licking my balls for the first time. With that encouragement, he really went to town. Sucking my balls in a way that made my dick jump with excitement. He worked his way back up the shaft, and then swallowed my cock again, his head bobbing up and down in my lap. I tried to hold back, to make it last as long as I could. But I was too fucking horny and Wade's mouth was too fucking hot.

I felt the first drops of precum leaking out of my dick. Wade must have tasted them, because he tried to pull his head back. But I grabbed him by the collar and held him down.

"Oh no you don't."

I kept a tight grip on his collar while I thrust my hips, fucking that beautiful face of his. Wade let out a muffled cry of protest, and then started to gag as my hot cum erupted against the back of his throat. But I didn't care. I held him down until I was good and done shooting my load into his mouth.

When it was over, I let go of his collar and leaned back in my chair, trying to catch my breath. Wade spat out my cum on the floor, coughing. And then he looked up at me with those big blue eyes.

I smiled at him and ran my fingers through his brown hair.

"Yeah. That's a good boy."

I stood up and stretched for a moment. And then I gestured for Wade to take the chair.

"Sit, boy."

Wade looked nervous, but he did as he was told. He settled into the chair, his rock-hard cock slapping against his stomach. And then I knelt down in front of him.

"What are you doing?" he asked, sounding a little scared.

"Whatever I want."

I began by licking his balls. I'd sure liked it, so I figured maybe Wade would too. He let out a surprised grunt and grabbed the sides of the chair. Slowly, I ran my tongue up the shaft of his cock. Unlike mine, his had a kind of curve to it. I could hear Wade's breathing getting faster, and I felt his legs start to tremble.

And then I got to the tip. Wade let out a little frightened whimper as my tongue explored the head of his dick. And then I slid it into my mouth.

Wade's whole body went tense, as I blew him for the first time. I'd imagined this a hundred times. But I hadn't expected the feeling of control. The way I could make Wade jump, or moan, or whimper.

It wasn't long before I tasted the first salty drops of precum, and realized that Wade was getting close. By now his whole body was shaking. I took his dick out of my mouth and wrapped my fingers around the slick shaft.

I only got in two good strokes before Wade cried out and started to cum. He gripped the arms of the chair as hard as he could and shot hot jizz all over his stomach and chest. Some of it even got into his hair. I kept my hand on his throbbing dick, pumping it over and over till he was good and empty, squeezing the last few drops of cum out of him. Finally, Wade collapsed back into the chair.

He looked down at me, exhausted.

"Good boy," I told him. "It's okay."

Wade leaned back, breathing heavily. His eyes closed. I got up quietly and went to get the last of my new toys.

When I came back, Wade seemed to be asleep. I knelt down to put the device on him.

"What are you doing?" Wade mumbled, as he felt the cold metal frame sliding down over his cock.

"Something to make you behave," I told him, as I closed the metal ring around the base of his balls, and snapped the lock shut.

Wade sat up and rubbed his eyes. He looked down at the device I'd locked him into. A tough metal and leather cage enclosing his limp cock, with a tight steel band around his balls to hold it in place.

"What the fuck is that?" he asked, suddenly awake.

"It's a cock cage," I told him, standing up.

He grabbed the thing and tried to pull it off his dick. But it wouldn't budge.

"How do I get this thing off?"

"*You* don't," I told him. "I've got the key."

Wade pulled on it harder, and let out a yelp as the metal ring bit into his balls.

"Ow! God damn it."

He started to panic. Tugging on it, twisting on it. Slowly realizing that he couldn't remove the cage without ripping his nuts off.

"Okay, enough fun and games Kevin. Get this thing off of me!"

I just smiled.

"No."

Wade grabbed the cock cage, pulling hard, grimacing in pain as the ring squeezed his balls. Until he couldn't take the pain anymore, and finally accepted that the cage wasn't coming off. With a terrified look on his face, Wade studied the leather and steel framework that was now firmly locked around his cock and balls.

"Seriously Kev, you can't do this! What's my girlfriend gonna think?"

"That she doesn't own your dick anymore."

And then another thought hit him.

"Oh my God! What about the guys? What are they gonna think when they see this? They'll crucify me!"

"Yeah," I agreed. "It's gonna be rough. Having a secret. Worried the football players will find out about it and rip you apart. I can sure see how that would be a bitch."

The irony of the situation was lost on Wade. He looked up at me, his blue eyes pleading.

"Come on, Kev. This wasn't part of the deal!"

"The deal?" I said. " The deal is that your goon squad is trying to beat the crap out of me. So now *that* stays on, until you find a way to make this right."

Part 3: The Cage

KEVIN

I spent the weekend catching up on homework and polishing my college applications. Maybe Wade could get into college just for tossing around a football, but I sure as Hell couldn't. I needed to dazzle the admissions boards with my essays. But the questions on the applications seemed intentionally stupid.

"What's your favorite word and why?"

"What is something about which you have changed your mind in the last three years?"

"Winston Churchill believed 'a joke is a very serious thing.' Tell us your favorite joke and try to explain the joke without ruining it."

Really? My entire future depends on whether or not I can explain a joke?

Well, at least I was having a better weekend than Wade. I kept imagining what he must going through, locked into that cock cage. All those thick metal bands around his dick. The leather straps holding them together. The tight steel ring under his balls locking the whole thing in place. Wade was probably going crazy trying to figure some way out of it. I just hoped he wasn't doing anything dangerous with power tools.

I wondered how horny he was getting. I have to jack off at least three times a day. If Wade was anything like me, he had to be ready to explode.

It was a little after four on Sunday that the doorbell rang. Mom went to get it.

"Uh... is Kevin home?"

My ears perked up at the sound of Wade's voice. He must be getting desperate to risk being seen outside my house in broad daylight.

"I'm sorry, Kevin is grounded," my mom told him. "And you are...?"

"I'm a friend of his. I... uh... really need to see him."

"About what?" my Mom asked.

Wade hesitated.

"Uh... you know. School stuff."

"Well, you can talk to him about it at school then."

Mom closed the front door and came back to my room. She looked me over suspiciously. I don't have many friends that come over to the house. And none of them had ever turned up wearing a varsity jacket.

"Kevin, do you want to tell me why Wade Johnson was at our front door?"

"Who?" I asked, trying to play dumb.

"Wade Johnson. The football quarterback?"

"Oh, yeah. Wade. I'm helping him with his schoolwork."

Mom raised an eyebrow.

"You're helping *Wade*? So you two are suddenly best buddies now?"

I smiled and tried to act cool.

"Yeah. He's having trouble passing English. I'm being nice."

"Nice?"

"Yeah. Nice."

"Right."

Mom had that look. She knew something was up.

"Wade isn't, maybe.... paying you to write term papers for him?"

I breathed a sigh of relief. Mom was on the wrong track.

"I gotta pay for college somehow," I told her. "Unless I have a trust fund you haven't told me about."

Mom studied my face, trying to decide if I was serious. Finally, she shrugged.

"Just don't get caught," she said, and left.

Whew.

I know that Mom and I are eventually gonna have that little chat about the fact that I like dick. But I'd rather do it as I'm walking out the door on my way to college.

Wade called me a couple minutes later. I got up and locked my bedroom door before I answered.

"Hey, Wade. How's it hanging?"

"Cute, Kev. You gonna let me out of this thing, now?"

"Have you told Logan and Tyler to leave me alone?"

"Dude, you know I can't do that!"

"Then *dude*, your dick is staying locked up."

"Come on!" Wade pleaded. "I've got a date with Brittany tonight. What am I going to do?"

"You could try talking to her," I suggested.

"Very funny."

Wade didn't say anything for a few seconds.

"So... uh... what time does your mom go to work today?" he finally asked.

"Why?"

"You know why. I'll come over and blow you. If you'll just take this damn thing off me."

My cock tingled at the suggestion. The thought of Wade on his knees. His mouth wrapped around my dick again. Those big blue eyes looking up at me. It took all the strength I had to say it.

"No."

"What!?"

Wade sounded surprised. Rejection was a new experience for him. I don't think he'd ever been turned down by a girl, let alone a guy.

"I thought you liked...?"

"Yeah, I do. But if I'm going to take a beating from your goons, then you're gonna have to do better than a blow job," I told him.

"What do you mean?"

"It's simple. Either you get Tyler and Logan off my ass. Or you give up yours."

There was a long silence.

"That's never gonna happen Kev."

"Then you and Brittany are going to have some nice long conversations."

"Fuck you, Kevin!" Wade shouted, and hung up.

I grinned and put down the phone. I ran my hand over the bulge in my jeans, and then unzipped them to give my cock a little breathing room. It was getting to the point where just the sound of Wade's voice was enough to get me hard. The difference was that I could do something about it. And poor Wade was just gonna get hornier and hornier. I wondered how long he could take it.

* * *

Monday it was back to the slow torture that is high school. And on top of the usual bullshit, I still had Logan to deal with. He hadn't cooled off over the weekend. He still had a big black eye, and he was still gunning for me. He and his buddy Tyler kept following me around, waiting for their chance to jump me. I managed to avoid getting a beat down by sticking close to teachers all day, but I couldn't keep that up forever.

At least Wade had lost a little of his cock-of-the-walk swagger. I saw his girlfriend arguing with him in the hallway, and at lunch she was giving him the cold shoulder. Apparently, she can be a real bitch when she's not getting any. Wade was trying to laugh it off, goofing around with his football posse. But there was a desperation in his eyes that he couldn't quite shake.

He started texting me after lunch.

We need to talk Kev.

Let's meet Kev.

Kev?

Kev!!! Answer me!!!

I let his frantic texts roll by. Wade was used to calling the shots. It was fun to make him sweat a little.

And besides, I couldn't set up a private meeting with him while Logan and Tyler were shadowing me everywhere. I tried everything I could think of to ditch them, but they were like a pair of fucking bloodhounds on my tail. I finally had to fake a stomach cramp in the middle of math. A little dramatic, but it got me a pass to the nurse's office while Logan and Tyler were busy in another class.

I texted Wade as I walked down the empty hallway.

"Meet me. Usual place. Now."

I went around to the back of the school and climbed up to the roof. I didn't have to wait long. Wade scrambled up the tree a couple minutes later. He caught sight of me and came running over.

"Kev! Great! Have you got the key for this thing?" he asked, grabbing his crotch.

"Nice to see you too, Wade."

So much for pleasantries. Wade unzipped his jeans and pulled out his cock. The steel rings of the cage were biting into it, holding his semi-hard dick in an iron grip. He must have had a rough couple of days.

Wade looked at me and forced a smile.

"Come on, Kev. You've had your fun. Now be a bro and get this thing off me."

I smiled back at him.

"No."

"But you have to!" Wade said, looking at me with big pleading eyes. "My girlfriend thinks that I'm cheating on her. And I can't even piss in front of the other guys. Do you know what they'll do to me if they see this thing?"

"Yep. Sure would be terrible to have a bunch of football players gunning for you."

"Great, so unlock this thing already!"

"That would be the irony thing again," I explained.

Wade looked confused.

"It's when you make a joke by saying the opposite of what you mean."

Wade scowled.

"It's not very funny."

"Depends on where you're standing," I said. "So you ready to call off Logan and Tyler?"

Wade shook his head.

"You know I can't do that! What the fuck would I tell them?"

"That I've got your balls in a vice?" I suggested.

"No way. If I start sticking up for you they'll think that I'm a fag, too."

"Fine," I said. "Hope you enjoy having a celibate senior year."

I turned to go, but Wade put a hand on my shoulder.

"No wait, Kev. Don't be that way."

Wade looked around to make sure we were alone, and then he pulled me close. I felt the steel rings around his cock brush against the leg of my jeans.

"There's... you know... other stuff I could do for you," Wade suggested.

He looked at me nervously. And then he reached down and pressed his palm up against my crotch. His hand was shaking, but he found my cock and grabbed it through the denim.

I shot him a surprised look. But Wade felt my dick getting hard, and took that as encouragement.

"Come on, Kev," he whispered, his breath hot in my ear. "Let me blow you."

I felt his hands fumbling with my belt, trying to undo the buckle. I looked down and saw his cock, all angry and red, desperately trying to get hard inside those steel rings. I was so horny that I couldn't think straight. But Wade was in even worse shape.

I reached around and grabbed his butt, pulling his body up against mine. Wade leaned against me, his face buried in my neck. I slid a hand inside his jeans and underwear, and ran it over the warm smooth skin of his ass. His dick gave a little jump, and a drop of his hot precum leaked onto the leg of my jeans. Maybe his cock couldn't get hard inside that cage, but it was sure as hell trying to.

I let my hand slide down the crack of his butt, until my fingers brushed against the tight little ring of his asshole.

"You ready to give that up now?" I asked, pressing a finger up against it.

"No, don't do that," Wade mumbled.

"Why? Afraid you might like it?" I asked, as the tip of my finger started to slip inside him.

But then Wade pushed me away, hard.

"What the fuck, Kev! I told you I can't do that. I'm not like you."

"Suit yourself," I said.

And then I left.

Let's see how Wade feels after a couple more days in the cock cage.

* * *

The next day, Logan and Tyler were still on the warpath. Following me around all over school, looking for their chance to jump me and deliver a beat down.

They almost got it. After third period I noticed that they weren't tailing me anymore. For a moment, I wondered if they'd finally given up. And then I realized what class I was heading to.

Gym.

They were gonna be waiting for me in the locker room. No adults around except for the PE teacher-- who is also the football coach. And it's not like he would bust a couple of his golden boy football players for beating up a fag.

So I cut PE and went to the library instead. If this kept up I'd have to forge a doctor's note or something. I started researching non-contagious diseases with no visible symptoms. Pancreatitis looked like it might fit the bill.

At least I had the pleasure of watching Wade squirm. His cheerleader girlfriend didn't even sit with him at lunch. The rest of his posse was still there, but the group dynamics seemed to be changing. Wade wasn't the cool confident center of attention anymore. Maybe the wolves were smelling weakness in him now.

I caught Wade looking at me once. I smiled back. And then I reached into my shirt and took out the little key that I was wearing on a chain around my neck. Wade stared at it for a few seconds before he realized what it was. Then his face turned all red and he looked away.

That's right, asshole. I may not have the key to your heart. But I've got the key to your dick. And I'm not going to let you forget it.

The rest of the school day was more of the same crazy dance. Me running from teacher to teacher. Logan and Tyler stomping along after me. The rest of the school taking bets on when they would finally beat my ass into the ground.

Somehow I managed to make it to the end of the day without getting my face bashed in. After school, I looked for Logan and Tyler in the parking lot, but they weren't waiting for me this time. So I grabbed my bag and started the jog home.

I really should not have underestimated those two. They may be dumb jocks, but they were determined. And it's not like my home address is a state secret.

The only thing that saved me was the red convertible. I spotted it as soon as I turned the corner on my block. Nobody on my street drives anything that expensive. So why the hell was there a bright red Mustang parked across from my house?

Something was up. I circled back around the block, cut across Mrs. Cleary's yard, climbed the back fence, and got into my house through the back door. And then I went around to the front windows and peeked out from behind the curtains.

Sure enough, Logan and Tyler were in the convertible. They were hunkered down, trying not to be spotted. But every minute or so they'd poke their heads up to see if I was coming. Apparently, they were pissed enough to cut football practice. This was getting serious. I called the police.

I'm a little fuzzy on the exact law, but I was under the impression that reporting a suspicious person lurking outside your home is supposed to get some kind of action. Twenty minutes later a cop finally turned up. He pulled up behind the convertible. Got out and walked over to talk to the occupants.

And then he saw their varsity jackets.

I hate Texas.

By the time the cop finished slapping Tyler and Logan on the back and congratulating them on their last win, I was ready to puke. After that, they all had a good laugh and the boys drove off. The cop jotted down something and then left a couple minutes later.

So much for the long arm of the law.

I was running out of options. Somehow, I had to convince Wade to get those two assholes off my case. But as it turned out, Wade was having football player problems of his own.

* * *

THE COACH

I was in my office, changing to go home when I heard the ruckus. I don't normally intervene in locker room shenanigans. Boys will be boys, and there's not much anybody can do about it. But this one sounded different. And besides, if the boys had this much energy left, then I hadn't kicked their butts hard enough during practice.

I poked my head out to see what was going on. Sure enough, four of my starting players were running around buck-naked, giving one of the other boys a good ribbing. They'd grabbed his clothes and were playing keep away with them. The weird thing was their choice of victim-- Wade Johnson, my star quarterback. Wade's normally dishing out the humiliation, not taking it.

"Someone want to tell me what's going on here?"

Thompson, my wide receiver, laughed. He held up Wade's jeans.

"Wade's gone fag on us," he said. "He's scared that if he showers with us he'll get a boner!"

Wade tried to snatch back his jeans, but Thompson danced out of his reach.

"I don't have time to shower today," Wade protested. "I gotta get home."

Wade made another grab for his jeans, but Martinez gave him a hard shove that knocked him back into the lockers.

What the hell was going on here? I looked them over. The other boys had all stripped naked, but Wade still had on his jockstrap from practice. And there was something weird about the shape of the bulge in it.

"Enough. You boys, hit the shower. Wade, my office."

The other players grabbed their towels and headed off to get cleaned up. Wade bent down to pick up his jeans.

"I'll just be a second, coach."

"*Now*, Wade."

Wade reluctantly dropped his jeans and followed me to my office. I closed the door. Wade stood there awkwardly, while I looked him over.

"Take off your jockstrap, Wade."

Wade looked terrified.

"Uh... I don't think..."

"*Now*, boy."

Wade swallowed hard, and slowly pulled off his jock strap. His cock was all locked up in a set of steel rings and leather straps.

Wade looked at me nervously, his face turning a deep red.

"My girlfriend... she's kind of kinky..." he stammered.

"Bullshit," I growled. "We both know that it wasn't a girl that locked you into that thing."

I shook my head in disappointment.

"Fuck. I wonder what your dad is going to say about this."

Wade's eyes went wide with terror.

"You can't! You can't tell my dad about this!" he pleaded.

"Can't imagine your girlfriend will be too happy either," I continued.

Wade's jaw began to tremble.

"And lord only knows what the rest of the team will do when they find out."

That was the last straw. Wade looked like he was gonna cry.

"Please," he begged. "You can't tell anyone."

I counted to ten, while I pretended to think about it. Just to let him sweat a little more. Wade was so scared he was shaking

"Maybe," I suggested. "Just maybe I could keep this between us."

Wade's eyes filled up with hope.

"But from now on you do everything I say. *Everything*. I fucking own your ass from now on. Understand?"

Wade nodded.

"Yeah, Coach. Anything you say."

I tossed him a pair of my gym shorts.

"Put those on."

Wade did as he was told. I walked past him and opened the door to the locker room.

"Don't fucking mouth off to me, Wade!" I yelled, loud enough for the other boys to hear. "Now get out there and give me twenty laps!"

That gave him an excuse for not showering with the rest of them. Wade nodded gratefully and headed back out to the field.

I took a few minutes to lock up my office, and then followed him. When I got to the field, I found Wade sitting on the bleachers talking to one of the cheerleaders. Figures.

"Hey! Johnson!" I barked at him. "I meant it about those laps! Get moving."

Wade looked like he was about to mouth off to me, but caught himself in time. He reluctantly got up and started jogging. With the same half-assed energy that he puts into everything else.

"Faster, Wade! I know that's not your top speed."

Wade grudgingly picked up the pace.

Wade's always been a frustration of mine. The boy has crazy talent. Arm like a rocket launcher and the accuracy of a sniper. But he's also lazy as

Hell. Everything has always come too fucking easy for him. But if I could get him to focus on his training, I might actually have something.

"Faster than that, Johnson!" I yelled again. He picked up the pace again. I was going to enjoy having leverage on him.

"Faster Johnson!"

Sweat was running down Wade's chest, and soaking into his shorts. I wondered just how far I could push him in other departments. I'd messed around with some of my players before. For gay boys in west Texas, there aren't a lot of sexual outlets. Getting fucked by their coach is a fantasy for half of them anyway. And if it gets them bumped up to first string? Everybody comes out a winner.

Usually, I can spot the gay boys on the team a mile off. I don't know how I missed Wade. From the look of that thing strapped around his cock, someone was already training him as a submissive. Breaking him, to use him any way they wanted. But who?

Wade came running up to me, out of breath.

"That's twenty," he said, barely able to get the words out.

"Good. Now give me five more."

Wade shook his head.

"I can't," he panted, struggling to catch his breath, "I've had it."

"You've had it if I tell your dad about that metal contraption on your dick. Now run!"

Wade wasn't happy about it, but he took off. Fighting to get around the field five more times. Pouring the last of his reserves into it. By the time he finished, he could barely stand.

"*Now* you're done," I told him.

I helped him back to the locker room, all sweaty and spent. The other boys were long gone.

"Now get cleaned up," I told him.

Wade slowly stripped off his sweaty shorts and then his jock strap. I tossed him a towel, and he shuffled off to the showers.

I stashed my own clothes in my office, and then joined him.

Wade was just standing there, too tired to move. Leaning against the wall with his head under the water. I turned on the shower next to him and started lathering up. Wade glanced over at me nervously. I soaped up my dick and gave it a few good strokes while he watched.

"You must miss jacking off," I said.

Wade didn't say anything, but his own dick turned red and pushed against the metal rings of its cage. Trying to get hard, but with no room for it. Wade grimaced.

"That thing hurt when you get excited?" I asked.

Wade nodded.

"Yeah," he mumbled. "It's like somebody squeezing my dick as hard as they can."

I reached over and felt the device. Solid steel rings connected by hard leather straps.

"You gonna tell me who put this on you?"

Wade avoided my eyes.

"I told you, Coach. It's Brittany. She doesn't like it when I mess around with other girls."

"And I told you that was bullshit. Or do you want me to ask her about it?"

Wade looked down and shook his head.

"I didn't think so."

I reached down and traced the steel band around the base of his balls that held the whole thing in place. As my fingers brushed his nuts, Wade shuddered, and I saw a drop of white precum leak from the head of his dick.

"Damn. How long has your master had you in this thing?" I asked.

Wade just stared at the floor.

I took him by the shoulders and turned him to face the wall. I could feel him shaking. I grabbed the soap and lathered up his back.

Wade stood there trembling, as my hands worked their way down. Soaping up his lower back. Then his ass. Till my fingers slid between his legs and brushed his tight little asshole.

"Don't do that," Wade mumbled softly.

"Why?" I asked. "Who are you saving your ass for?"

"No one," Wade stammered. "I'm not like that."

"Bullshit," I said, kicking his legs apart. "You're somebody's bitch."

I slapped his ass with my hard dick, just to let him know what he was in for. Wade panicked. He tried to turn around, but I shoved him up against the wall and pinned him there.

"You want me to tell your dad about that metal thing on your dick?" I growled into his ear.

"No, sir."

"Then stop your squirming."

I pressed my big cock up against his tight little asshole. Wade wriggled around in my arms but I held him tight, his muscular body soapy and slick against mine. And then the fat head of my dick popped inside him.

Wade let out a surprised little cry like he'd never felt such a thing before.

"Shh..." I whispered in his ear. "If you can take it from your master, you can take it from your coach."

I slid another inch of my cock inside him. Wade groaned and clenched his teeth. He was so fucking tight that his asshole felt like a rubber band stretched around my dick.

"Come on, Wade. You know how to do this. If you don't relax it's gonna hurt like hell."

I stroked Wade's stomach, slowly coaxing him into calming down and loosening up. The boy was acting like he'd never been fucked before. Maybe his master had a tiny dick. Or maybe Wade just likes to play the virgin. It could be part of the game for him.

I held him tight in my arms, using my voice to keep him calm, while I slowly worked my dick into that tight ass of his. Feeling him squirm and whimper as he struggled to take it. Until finally I felt his ass ring clenched around the base of my cock, and my nuts brushing up against his ass.

"Yeah. That's it, boy."

I started fucking him, slow and deep. But I only got in a few good pokes before Wade let out a howl. He thrashed around in my arms, as his dick made a final effort to break out of its cage. And then he was cumming, screaming as he shot his hot jizz all over the shower wall. Jesus. The boy must have been saving that one up for a while. I've never seen anyone shoot so much.

When it was over, Wade looked back over his shoulder at me. The water dripping down from his curly hair, his big blue eyes confused. Like he didn't understand what had just happened.

"Oh no," I told him. "I'm not done with you, Johnson"

And then I gave him the fucking he deserved. Hard and fast. Pounding that cute little ass like a jackhammer. Wade braced himself against the wall, moaning and wailing and making all kinds of a fuss. Trying to act like he'd never been used that way before.

I fucked him good and hard until I couldn't hold back anymore. I slammed my cock into him a final time, and Wade let out a little cry as he felt my hot cum erupting inside him. And then all of a sudden Wade was cumming-- again. He threw his head back against me as he shot a second load of jizz out all over the shower tiles. Wow. The boy might be on a hair-trigger, but he was quick on the reload, too.

When Wade was done shaking, I slowly pulled my dick out of him. Wade let out a final whimper, and then collapsed back against me. I held him up, the hot water still pouring over us, while he caught his breath.

"Now say it," I whispered in his ear. "Who owns your ass from now on?"

Wade lifted his head and looked back at me. He swallowed hard. But he said it.

"You do, coach."

"Damn straight I do."

* * *

KEVIN

The situation with Logan and Tyler was getting out of hand. Chasing me around school was one thing. But turning up outside my house? That was fucked up. How far were they gonna push this?

Well, I wasn't going to make it easy for them. After mom went to work I made sure the house was secure. I checked the locks on all the windows, and I retrieved the spare key from the fake rock in the front yard. And then I sat down for a long session with my old friend Amazon to start pricing tasers.

I almost jumped out of my skin when the front doorbell rang. I glanced at the clock. 9:15. A little late for girl scouts or Jehovah's witnesses.

I walked quietly to the door and looked through the peephole. I had a minor panic attack when I spotted the varsity jacket. But then he turned around and I saw who it was.

I opened the door.

"Wade? What are you doing here?"

Wade just stood there, staring at the ground. I waited for him to say something, but he didn't seem to be in a talkative mood.

"Well?"

"I um. . . I uh . . ."

I waited for him to finish the thought, but his brain seemed to have stalled.

"Did you know that your goon squad tried to jump me on my way home today?"

Wade looked up at me. And for a second I thought he was actually worried.

"Did they hurt you?"

"Not this time."

Wade studied my face, like he was trying to make up his mind about something. Then he pushed his way past me into the house.

"Nice to see you, too," I said.

I closed the door and locked it. Wade stood in the hall, his hands stuffed in his varsity jacket.

"So are you gonna tell me why you're here?"

Wade looked down at his feet for a while.

"I'll do it," he finally said.

I let out a sigh of relief. It was over.

"Great. Have you told Logan yet? Can you get him and Tyler off my back before school tomorrow?"

Wade looked confused.

"No," he said. "I . . . uh . . . I mean the other thing."

It took me a second to understand what he was saying. I walked over and stood in front of him. His face just a couple of inches from mine.

"You mean the other thing where *I fuck you*?"

Wade's face turned red, and he bit his lip. He looked back at me and nodded slowly.

"Then say it," I told him.

"I'll..... I'll let you fuck my ass," he stammered. "If you'll just take this damn thing off my dick."

I could hear the desperation in Wade's voice. He meant it. After four days in the cock cage, he must have reached his breaking point.

"Okay. Come on then," I told him.

I led him back to my bedroom, feeling a little light-headed. After all the times that I'd imagined this, it didn't seem quite real.

I got Wade's collar out from under my bed.

"On your knees."

Wade made a face and muttered something under his breath, but he knelt down in front of me. I strapped the thick leather collar around his neck.

"Good boy," I said, running my fingers through his hair.

Wade looked up at me with his blue eyes. I thought about making him blow me, but I was too impatient to get to the main event.

"Get naked," I ordered him.

Wade stood up. He slowly stripped down, his face bright red. He got down to his underwear and hesitated. He looked at me nervously for a few seconds, and then finally shucked them off. He stood there, naked except for his dog collar-- and the leather and steel cage around his dick.

"Now get your ass in my bed."

Wade looked at me and swallowed hard. He laid down on his stomach and buried his face in my pillow. Like he didn't want to see what was coming.

I grabbed the lube out of my desk and crawled into bed next to him. I ran a hand over his warm smooth ass. I could feel him trembling.

I wasn't sure how this next part was supposed to go. It looks easy in porn films. You lube up your cock and stick it right in a guy's ass. But those porn guys are pros, and Wade was a virgin. I figured his tight little ass might need a little coaxing before it was ready to take its first dick.

"Roll over, boy."

Wade did as he was told, turning over onto his back. He looked up at me with big scared eyes as I pushed his legs apart. I uncapped the lube and poured some into my hand. And then I reached between his legs and ran my oily fingers over his tight little asshole.

Wade stared at the ceiling, bracing himself for what was coming. I played with the rim of his slick asshole for a few seconds, and then slid a finger inside. Wade grimaced, like it hurt a little. And then my finger brushed up against something inside him.

All of a sudden Wade gasped for breath and his eyes went wide. His dick twitched inside its cage, turning red and angry.

Well, that was interesting. I slid my finger back out, and then tried stroking the same spot again.

Wade's dick jerked to life. He stared at it, confused. Like he couldn't understand why it was behaving that way. It flopped around on his stomach, trying to break out of its cage, and then leaked hot precum. Wade closed his eyes and moaned.

Looks like I found Captain Cool's Achilles heel.

I slowly finger fucked Wade. He thrashed around on the bed. Grabbing the sheets and balling up his fists, trying to control himself.

When he seemed to be handling one finger okay, I tried slipping in two. Wade whimpered and threw his head back. I saw the ring around his balls tighten as his dick strained against the cage, trying to break free. He arched his back, and his abs rippled with every thrust of my fingers.

I kept it up until I figured he was good and ready.

Wade opened his eyes as he felt my fingers slide out of him. He watched as I unbuttoned my jeans and pulled out my dick. I took one of his hands and wrapped it around my boner.

"Think about what *that's* going to feel like inside you."

Wade eyed it nervously. There's a big difference between having a couple of fingers inside you and a nine-inch dick.

I grinned back at him. And then I looked up and caught sight of us in the mirror on my closet door. Skinny little me with my huge dick kneeling over big old muscular Wade.

I wanted him to see it too.

"Get up boy. I want you on your hands and knees."

Wade did as he was told. He rolled over and got up on all fours, like a dog. I pointed him at the mirror so that he'd have to watch. And then I knelt behind him and oiled up my dick.

I thought about all the times I'd gotten a hard-on seeing Wade in gym class. All the times he'd picked on me and called me a faggot. All the time I'd spent hating him and wanting him in the worst way, dreaming of having him naked in my bed and ready to take it. But I never thought in a million years it would actually happen.

I oiled up the head of my dick, and then pressed the slick head up against the tight ring of his asshole. Wade started to pull away, but I grabbed his collar and yanked him back.

"You've been riding my ass for years, Wade. So you can fucking take it from me for a change."

Wade let out a little yip as the head of my cock slid inside him. He opened his mouth, gasping for air.

"That's it," I whispered to him. "Good boy."

I let him have a few seconds to catch his breath. And then I gave him the rest of it. Wade lowered his head, struggling to take it as inch after inch of my oily cock slowly slipped inside him. Clenching his teeth as my dick stretched his tight cherry ass to the limit.

Wade let out a cry as the last inch of my dick slid into him. He raised his head and saw his reflection in the mirror. And then he quickly looked away.

"Oh no," I said, grabbing him by the hair. "I want you to see this."

I held Wade's head up and made him watch while I fucked him. Long deep thrusts that made his eyes roll up in his head. And then harder and faster, till Wade broke out in a sweat, till he was panting and whimpering like a little dog. I wanted him to remember this image the next time he called someone a faggot. I wanted him to remember being on all fours with my dick inside him.

I fucked him till I was out of breath and we were both covered in sweat. And I still wanted more. I wanted to have Wade's ass every way I could.

Wade shuddered as I pulled my dick out of him. He looked back at me, wondering if it was over.

"Get on your back," I told him. "I want to fuck you missionary."

While Wade flipped over I pulled off my sweat-drenched T-shirt and kicked off my shoes. I shucked off my jeans and underwear, and then turned back to see Wade looking up at me. He had the weirdest expression on his face.

It's funny. In spite of everything I'd done with Wade, I'd never gotten completely naked in front of him before. I guess I was a little nervous about being the skinny geek next to the golden boy jock. And yet, there was Wade, looking up at me like a starving man staring at a slab of steak.

And then I realized what it was. He was looking at the key on the chain around my neck.

"Is this what you want, boy?" I asked, holding it up.

Wade nodded.

"Yeah."

"Then earn it. Get those legs in the air."

Wade didn't understand, so I grabbed his ankles and showed him what I wanted.

"Like that. Now hold them there."

Wade looked at me uncertainly, and then tucked his hands behind his knees.

"Good boy."

I pushed his knees apart. And then I guided my cock back into Wade's warm waiting ass. He tensed up for a moment, and then threw his head back and let out a moan.

"There you go," I said, "you're getting the hang of it."

I fucked him slowly for a while, watching his face react to each thrust of my dick. His big blue eyes staring right into mine.

I reached down and felt the cage on his cock. Traced the tight steel band around his nuts that was holding it in place.

"You want me to let you out?"

Wade's eyes filled with hope.

"Yes," Wade begged. "Please."

I took the chain off my neck and lowered the key down to the lock.

"One last thing. Who owns your ass, boy?"

Wade glared at me.

"If you want your cock back, you're gonna have to say it."

I ran my fingers over his balls. Wade groaned and closed his eyes. He didn't want to say it. But after four days in the cage, he couldn't take it anymore.

"You do, Kev," he blurted out. "You own my ass."

"And don't forget it."

I unlocked the cage.

Given how horny Wade was, I expected it to shoot off and fly across the room. But the metal rings were so tight around his semi-hard cock that it was kind of stuck. I lubed it up and pulled on it, and finally managed to slide it off

Wade gave a sigh of relief, as his dick slapped down on his stomach and filled out to a rock-hard boner. He took his right hand off his leg and started to reach for it. But I slapped his hand away.

"Did I say you could touch yourself, boy?"

Wade was so frustrated that I thought he was going to cry. But then I grabbed his dick and gave it a nice slow stroke.

"Oh God!" Wade moaned.

And then I gave him the fucking he's always deserved. Pounding his tight ass while I jacked him off at the same time. Wade arched his back, beads of sweat rolling off his chest. He looked up at me, his lower lip trembling. He put his hand on the back of my neck and pulled my face down to his, his blue eyes looking into mine.

And then he kissed me.

I wasn't expecting it. All of a sudden his lips were against mine and his tongue was in my mouth. And then I was cumming, shooting hot jizz all up inside Wade's ass.

Wade must have felt it. He moaned into my mouth, and then he was cumming too, shooting all over his stomach.

It seemed to go on forever. When it was finally over, I collapsed on top of him, sweating and panting. Wade put an arm around me, and I could feel his chest heaving underneath me.

Eventually, I recovered enough to pull my dick out of him. Wade let out a little grunt as it popped out. And then I rolled off him.

We lay next to each other for a while, catching our breath. And then I guess I must have passed out for a while. When I woke up, Wade was getting dressed. He pulled on his clothes in silence. And then he picked up his Varsity jacket and walked out of my room without saying anything. A few seconds later I heard him leave by the front door.

I buried my head in my pillow.

This was totally fucked up.

Part 4: The Coach's Boy

KEVIN

It was a good thing that I woke up early. Wade had left my bedroom door open, and his dog collar and cock cage lying out in plain sight. I hid them under my bed before mom got home from work. Lord knows that would have been an awkward conversation.

I showered and got ready for school. Over breakfast, Mom droned on about some drama she was having with a coworker. I nodded politely, but my mind was on other things. I was still trying to figure out what had happened last night.

I mean, I knew what had *happened*. --I'd fucked Wade Johnson! It still didn't seem quite real. The jock who's been making my life hell for the last two years had been naked in my bed with my dick inside him.

And he liked it!

That was the crazy thing. Okay, it probably helped that I'd had his cock locked up in a chastity device for a week, and the jerk had so much pent-up cum that he was ready to explode. But still, it made me wonder. With the right training, would every straight jock learn to like getting fucked? At any rate, it had been one hell of a way to lose my virginity.

But now I felt a little empty, knowing that it was over. Wade and I were even now, and he was off the hook. He could go back to screwing his girlfriend. And I probably wouldn't get laid again until college.

There was just one thing that I couldn't figure out-- *the kiss*. That moment when Wade grabbed the back of my neck, looked into my eyes, and kissed me. What the hell was that about? It kept gnawing at me.

Maybe Wade had done it just to screw with me. I got to fuck with his ass, so he decided to fuck with my head. Plant a good kiss on the faggot, and let him wonder about it for the rest of his life.

Except . . . Wade isn't that clever. He wouldn't think of something like that. Especially not in the middle of getting his cherry popped, with my dick pounding away inside him.

So it must have been a reflex. Wade's in the habit of kissing girls during sex, so he'd kissed me, too. It probably didn't mean anything.

But it sure felt like it meant something last night.

When I got to school, Logan and Tyler were waiting near my locker, snickering about something. With everything that had happened, I'd forgotten about those two. They were still waiting for a chance to deliver on that beatdown that they'd promised me.

Well, I knew that they weren't going to jump me in the middle of the hallway with teachers watching. So I walked right past them and opened my locker. If I'd been paying attention, I would have noticed the puddle. But instead, I just reached in like an idiot and grabbed my book for first period.

"What the fuck?"

My history book was sopping wet. And it smelled. Like urine. Everything in my locker was soaked. And I was standing in a puddle of it.

I heard Logan and Tyler bust out laughing behind me. And they weren't alone. There was a whole crowd, staring at me holding my wet textbook.

"Jesus Kevin, your locker stinks," Logan said.

I just stood there, my face burning red, while they all had a good laugh. And then the bell for first period rang. Not sure what else to do, I dropped my book and stumbled off to history.

I managed to make it through the first few minutes of class without a problem. But then Ms. Carpenter told us to open our textbooks and turn to chapter five. So I had to sit there awkwardly until she noticed that I didn't have my book with me. And when she asked about it, the whole class started giggling. Apparently, the story of my locker being turned into a urinal was getting around. I sat there for the rest of class, wishing I could disappear. Hearing the whispers and the chuckling behind me.

When the end-of-class bell finally rang, I headed for the school office. I told the secretary that I needed a new set of textbooks. When I told her *why* I needed them, she wrinkled her nose.

"Maybe you should see the principal about that?"

"Sure."

I waited for ten minutes while the principal wrapped up a phone call, and then went into his office. After I gave him the details, he ran a hand through his thinning hair.

"Ugh. Kevin, that's a few hundred dollars worth of books. I can have Cheryll get you new copies. But you're going to have to pay for the ones you lost."

"What?!"

He shrugged.

"School rules. You're responsible for . . ."

"Fuck that!" I yelled at him.

The principal looked at me in shock. I was a little surprised too. But my mouth was running faster than my brain.

"A football player pisses on my books, and *I'm* the one who has to pay to replace them? Are you kidding me?"

"The books were in your possession, Kevin. It was your job to keep them safe and return them at the end of the semester."

"No," I told him, leaning over his desk. "There is no fucking way in hell that I am paying for this!"

The principal stood up and got right in my face.

"That bit of profanity just earned you detention, mister. We're done."

He sat back down.

Fuck.

I turned and stormed out. There is no fucking justice in this world. At least not in Texas.

I killed time in the hall, waiting for second period to end. I wanted to go home. Run away from this place and never come back. Anything besides facing another day with these assholes.

The bell rang, and I trudged off to my third-period computer class. All along the way, groups of kids pointed at me and snickered. Apparently, the whole school had heard by now. And then a big crowd of varsity jackets blocked my way.

"What's that smell?" Logan said. "New cologne, Kevin?"

"I'll bet all the other queers love it!" chimed in Tyler.

They all had a good laugh at that. I glared at them, wishing I had Superman's heat vision and could incinerate the whole lot of them.

And that's when I saw Wade. Standing there, laughing along with all the rest of them. I couldn't believe it. I just stared at him, my mouth hanging open.

Logan elbowed Wade.

"Look at that! I think the queer is offering you a blowjob. You want to stick your dick in there?"

Wade looked at me and shook his head.

"Fucking faggot," he said softly.

I thought my head was going to explode. I just stared at him, while they all laughed at me. And then the bell rang and they all hurried off to class.

I couldn't bring myself to show my face in computer class, so I went and hid in the library. I found a place in the back of the stacks where I could be alone. And then I sat down and hugged my knees to my chest.

This was never going to end. Those assholes were going to keep ruining my life, every single day. Just because they could.

And Wade . . . Why the fuck had I thought that Wade was any different? I could feel something welling up inside me. I wasn't sure if I was going to cry, or scream, or . . .

. . . get even. Yeah. *That's* what I was going to do.

I sent Wade a text.

"I think it's time the football team finds out that I'm not the only faggot in this school."

I attached a video. A little something from our second night together. Wade's striptease for me. His naked lap dance. The big finish with his lips wrapped around my cock.

My camera placement hadn't been good and the angle was lousy. But you could tell that it was Wade, and you could tell that it was me. And you could tell what he was doing to me.

Nothing happened for a while. And then third period ended and Wade checked his messages. The responses came fast and furious.

Dude! You said you didn't film that!

You can't show that to anybody!

Please don't show that to anybody!

I'll do anything! What do you want?

Talk to me Kev! What do you want?

I let the frantic texts roll by for a few minutes, savoring Wade's desperation. And then I sent a reply.

"That video goes live at the end of the school day, asshole. You're about to be famous."

I wanted Wade to know what was coming. I wanted him to spend the whole day waiting for it, knowing that his world was about to come crashing down. And that there was nothing he could do about it this time.

Wade sent a few more frantic texts, but I turned off my phone without reading them. Much as I enjoyed having Wade beg, I didn't want him to weaken my resolve.

The truth is that I was terrified. I was about to blow up my whole fucking world, and I had no idea where the pieces would land. What would it be like, going to a school where everyone had seen a sex tape of me and the star quarterback? It didn't seem like things couldn't get any worse for me. But I was about to find out.

And what about Mom? This isn't how I'd planned on coming out to her. I was pretty sure that she wouldn't actually watch the video. But she'd hear about it, and she'd know that everyone else in town had. All her friends. Everyone in line at the store. All the folks giggling behind her back at work.

I wondered what she'd do about it. Mom's not overly religious, but we've never talked about the gay thing. For all I know, she might ship me off for some kind of crazy "de-gaying" treatment.

But I had to do something. I couldn't just sit here and take it for one more day. Something had to change.

I hid there in the back of the library for the next few periods. My stomach in knots. Dreading what I was about to unleash.

The librarian finally found me during sixth period and made me go to class. Chemistry actually turned out to be a welcome distraction. And then it was seventh period and AP Economics. But halfway through class, the secretary came by with a message.

Mr. Hathaway read it and shrugged.

"Kevin, the principal wants to see you in his office."

"What for?" I asked.

"Didn't say. Just go."

I got up and walked to the office. I figured it had something to do with the new textbooks. But when I got there, the principal had a surprise for me.

"Kevin, this is Wade Johnson. He wants to try and resolve this friction you're having with the football team."

I stared at Wade dumbly.

"He does?"

"Yeah Mr. Baxter," Wade said, flashing his thousand-watt smile. "It's all a big misunderstanding. I'm sure we can work it out. Could we maybe have the office for a few minutes?"

"Fine," the principal said, picking up a few papers from his desk. "Just get this situation taken care of."

The principal left, closing the door behind him.

I turned to Wade in disbelief.

"So you can just take over the Principal's office?" I asked. "Is there anything they won't let you do at this school?"

"You didn't give me any choice! What the hell are you doing, Kev?"

"I'm taking the target off my ass and putting it on yours!" I told him. "Let's see what your football buddies do when they find out that I'm not the only cocksucker in this school."

"But you told me you weren't filming that!" he said.

Wade seemed genuinely hurt by the betrayal.

"No," I corrected him. "I told you that my laptop was in the other room. I didn't say anything about wireless webcams or . . ."

I stopped. It sounded stupid, even to me.

"Okay, so I'm an asshole too," I admitted. "But you fucking deserve it!"

Wade put a hand on my shoulder.

"You gotta calm down, Kev. You can't show that video to anyone."

I slapped his hand away.

"Oh yes I can! It goes live at three o'clock, right when everyone is checking their cell phones after school. Have fun at football practice, asshole."

Wade glanced at the clock. Only an hour left. He was trying to keep it together, but fear was starting to get the best of him.

"Seriously, Kev. I know you're pissed. But you don't want to do this."

"Oh yes I do!"

"Do you have any idea what the guys will do to me if they see that?"

"Yeah! The exact same things that you've all been doing to me every day for the last three years!"

"You can't, Kev! You're gonna fuck up my whole life!" Wade pleaded.

"And what about my life!" I shouted back. "Does my life count for nothing just because I can't throw a fucking football?"

Wade shrugged. Yeah, in Texas that's exactly how it works.

"Fuck that," I told him. "You're going down."

Wade looked at me with his big blue eyes. I could see tears starting to well up.

"You really hate me this much, Kev?"

"Dude! Your idiot friends just pissed in my locker!"

"And what am I supposed to do about it?"

"Tell them to fucking back off! Tell them it's not cool! Do anything besides stand there laughing and calling me a *faggot*!"

A tear ran down Wade's cheek.

"I don't get it, Kev. I've called you a faggot like a million times since tenth grade. Why does this one time suddenly matter so much more?"

"Because . . . well . . . because . . ."

I stammered on, trying to figure it out. Why did I expect something more from Wade? It's not like we were friends. Why did I think that anything had changed just because I'd fucked him?

I looked at Wade. The tussled hair. The tears trickling down his face. So much for the big tough jock. And maybe I didn't really hate him enough to do this.

"I'll let you fuck me again," he said softly.

Damn it. Wade knew how to play me. But I was still furious with him.

"I've already had your ass," I reminded him.

"Yeah. But you liked it, right?"

I didn't say anything. There was a cold knot of anger in my gut that still wanted revenge. Not just on Wade, but on the whole fucking football clique that runs this school. I wanted to walk up to Logan and Tyler and say,

"Yeah, I'm a faggot. I'm the faggot who's been fucking your golden boy quarterback, you dumbwads!"

Wade watched me thinking it over. He put his arm around my shoulders and pulled me closer.

"Come on, Kev," he pleaded, his face just a few inches from mine. "I'll do anything you want. I'll be your fucking slave. Just *please* don't do this."

I wrestled with my feelings for a few more seconds.

"My *slave*," I repeated back to him. "*Anything* I fucking want? I own you?"

Wade nodded.

"Yeah. Anything you want, Kev."

I looked into Wade's eyes. Remembered the feeling of having him underneath me. Moaning and writhing. The look on his face when I came inside him. Damn it, I couldn't say no. But I still wanted to make him squirm.

"Okay," I said.

I sat down behind the Principal's desk and unzipped my jeans.

"Blow me."

Wade's eyes went wide.

"Jesus, Kev! Put that away! What if someone walks in?"

"Then they're gonna see you on your knees with my dick in your mouth. Or we can wait and let the whole school see that video at three. Which one is it going to be?"

Wade glanced nervously at the door. He was terrified of getting caught. But he was out of options. He knelt down in front of me. And then he slowly slid my cock between his lips.

Fuck. I'm not sure what was better. The feeling of Wade's warm wet mouth on my dick, or the feeling that I'd *won*. I almost wanted the principal to walk in on us. He lets the football team run this fucking school. So let him get a good look at how I'm using his star player.

I let out a moan, as Wade slid his tongue over the head of my dick. He was getting better with practice. I ran my fingers through his curly brown hair, while he struggled to get me off as fast as he could. He looked up at me, watching to see what I liked.

He got me close so fast that I barely had time to enjoy it. But I made sure he learned his lesson this time. I grabbed his hair and held his head down while I face fucked him.

"And.. I . . . want . . . you . . . to . . . remember . . . this," I said, ramming my cock into his mouth over and over again. "The next time you want to call me a *faggot!*"

And then I came. Wade grimaced and made a funny sound as my hot jizz erupted into his mouth, but he took it.

When it was over, I leaned back in the Principal's chair, catching my breath. I could get used to this. Wade made a face and looked around for someplace to spit. But I think he realized that leaving a mouthful of cum on the office floor might raise some questions.

Suddenly, there was a knock at the door. Wade jumped to his feet, and I hurriedly shoved my dick back in my pants. The door opened and the Principal stuck his head in.

"Have you boys got everything straightened out?"

I stood up and grinned at him.

"Yes sir. I think we've got it settled. Right Wade?"

Wade nodded, without saying anything. He couldn't talk with a mouthful of cum, and apparently he was too chicken shit to swallow.

The principal came in and reclaimed his chair.

"Great. Then I don't want to hear any more about this nonsense."

I started to go. But I was feeling cocky. I turned back to the principal.

"Oh, there is just *one* more thing, sir."

The principal sighed.

"What is it now, Kevin?"

"I'm not paying for the new textbooks. Wade and I decided that since Logan and Tyler destroyed my last set, they should pay for them. Right Wade?"

Wade glared at me, but kept his cum-filled mouth shut. The principal groaned.

"Or you could just take it out of the athletic budget," I suggested helpfully.

The principal looked at me with tired eyes and gestured to the door.

"Just get out of my office, you two."

Out in the hall, Wade ran to the water fountain to spit. I chuckled as he wiped his lips and tried to wash the taste out of his mouth.

"That was just round one," I reminded him. "I'm going to expect a hell of a lot more from you tonight, slave boy."

Wade looked at me, and nodded slowly.

"Yeah. I'll be there, Kev. Just keep *your* promise."

And then the bell rang, and I headed off to my last class of the day. Suddenly, high school was looking a whole lot better.

* * *

THE COACH

I walked out to the field to start practice. It was one of those perfect days. Blue sky, fresh cut grass, and a team full of randy boys in uniform for me to whip into shape.

And best of all, there was Wade. Who would have guessed that my star quarterback was secretly a submissive little bottom boy? For all his cocky bluster, Wade just needed to be fucked and dominated. And now that I owned his ass, I could finally force him to buckle down and focus on his training. --Both on the field and bent over my desk. Yep, this was gonna be one hell of a season.

The boys were horsing around, in high spirits. I blew the whistle to start practice.

"Playtime's over ladies. For the next two hours, your asses belong to me."

I had them line up and stretch. Wade kept talking, some crazy story about a girl he'd fucked over the summer.

"Fascinating Johnson. But we're here to play football. So shut up and stretch those hamstrings."

Wade grinned. He bent over. --And then turned to Tyler and finished telling the story.

I should have known it wouldn't be so easy. All through practice, Wade kept pulling the same bullshit that he always does. Joking around with the guys when he should have been focusing on the game. Doing every drill half-assed. Relying on natural talent over effort.

I wanted to bend him over my knee and spank him. But maybe that was the point, part of Wade's little game as a submissive. Play the cocky bad boy now, so that I have to punish him later. Well, I could play that game, all right.

I was still trying to figure Wade out. After seeing that crazy leather contraption locked around his dick, I knew that he was into some kind of bondage play. But I wouldn't be able to use him the way I wanted to until I knew *exactly* how to push his buttons.

"Okay, good work everybody," I said, calling an end to practice. "Hit the showers."

But as they turned to go, I grabbed Wade by the shoulder.

"Not you, Chatty Cathy. Your lazy ass is going to give me twenty laps."

Wade looked at me like I was crazy.

"But Coach . . ."

"Keep mouthing off, and it will be thirty," I barked at him.

Wade grumbled, but headed back towards the field.

I followed the rest of the boys inside. While they horsed around in the locker room, I sat down at my desk and mulled over the Wade situation. He was going to take more work than I'd thought. But it was going to be worth it. Wade, properly broken and trained, would be one hell of a player. --And an even better fuck slave.

My thoughts were interrupted by a knock on my office door.

"Coach?"

It was Danny, my second-string quarterback. He was standing in the doorway, wearing nothing but his jockstrap from practice. Danny is blond, and toned, and cute as a button. Not very well-liked by the other players, though. From what I hear, the fact that he's fucked all their girlfriends might have something to do with it. In his way, he's even cockier than Wade.

But Danny's also short-- five feet even. And that's his problem.

Danny's dad moved his family into our district a couple years ago, in the hopes of getting his son on a better team. He's convinced that Danny is going to be the next Peyton Manning. But Danny's just too damn short for that. It's basic mechanics: A tall quarterback can see over the opposing players, and find the openings. And longer arms give a taller player better mechanical advantage, which means longer passes. The ideal quarterback is someone like Wade, 6'5 or taller.

Still, little blond Danny standing there in his jockstrap was a pleasant sight. I couldn't help but smile.

"You got a minute, coach?"

"Sure, Danny. What's on your mind?"

"It looked like you were having trouble with Wade today."

"He can be a handful," I admitted.

"You should give me a chance. Let me show you what I can do."

"I should?"

"Yeah. I worked hard all summer. I'm a lot better than I was last season."

Maybe kid. But you haven't grown a foot.

"I'll think about it," I told him.

"Okay."

Danny started to go. And then he turned back to me.

"Is there anything I can do, Coach? You know, to improve my chances?"

He said it innocently enough. And it was the sort of question any player might ask. But they wouldn't ask it standing in my office in a jockstrap.

I looked Danny over with more interest. If the rumors were true, he'd fucked his way through most of the cheerleading squad last year. Not bad for a guy who rode the bench all season. But sometimes the gay boys are the biggest pussy hounds. Like they've got something to prove. Or maybe Danny was straight, and just willing to go the extra mile.

"What did you have in mind?" I asked.

"I don't know," Danny said, scratching his chin. As he lowered his hand he let it brush against the bulge in his jockstrap.

I tried not to make it obvious, but he saw my eyes lingering.

"Maybe I could stay late, Coach?" he suggested. "Do some extra training?"

Danny was definitely testing the waters. I wondered just how far he was willing to go. I knew the kind of training I wanted to give him. Teaching him how to handle my cock in his ass. Seeing the look in his eyes the first time I came inside him.

Yeah. Any other year, I could have had some fun with Danny. But I was already training Wade. Fucking two of my players at once would be greedy. --And risky.

"Thanks, Danny. But I'm busy today. Wade and I are running some drills later."

Danny looked confused.

"You sure, coach? 'Cause Wade just hit the showers."

"What the . . .?"

Wade should have been running those laps for another half hour. I got up and pushed my way past Danny.

Sure enough, Wade was in the showers, horsing around with the other guys.

"Johnson!" I barked at him. "I thought I had you running laps?"

Wade flashed an "awe-shucks" grin at me.

"I can't today coach. I got a date with my girl."

And then he turned back to the other boys. I watched him, laughing and joking around with the guys. His dick swinging free, just like theirs.

So that was it. Wade's master had let him out of that cock cage. And now Wade figures that I can't tell anyone about it.

"Grab a towel, Johnson. I want you in my office. Now!"

I got to my desk and waited, fuming, while Wade took his sweet time drying off. Finally, he came and stood in the doorway.

"Yeah, what is it, coach?"

I growled at him in a low voice.

"You swore to me that I owned your ass, boy."

Wade stared at me blankly.

"I don't know what you mean, Coach."

"Yesterday, after practice. We made a deal. I promised not to tell anyone about your little faggot bondage games. And you swore to me that I owned your ass."

Wade shrugged.

"I don't know what you're talking about Coach. Anyway, I gotta go. Late for my date."

Wade turned and walked off.

So that's how he was going to play it. Just pretend like the whole thing had never happened.

Fine, Wade. Go ahead and fuck your girlfriend. But this is not over.

You broke your promise. So now I'm going to break *you*.

* * *

KEVIN

Wade got to my house at 8 pm sharp. If nothing else, I was teaching him punctuality. He looked at me nervously as I opened the door.

"Hey Kev! So . . . are you still pissed at me?"

"Get your ass in here," I told him.

I led him into the kitchen. Wade saw the hardwood paddle lying on the table.

"Not that thing!" he protested. "Isn't it enough that I'm gonna let you fuck me?"

I grabbed him by the collar of his varsity jacket.

"Let's get one thing straight, Wade: you don't *let* me do anything. You're my slave. I own you, and I can use you any fucking way I want to. That's the deal. Now strip down and get ready for it."

Wade took another look at the paddle. He started taking off his clothes, very slowly. Trying to delay his punishment.

"Some time today, Wade."

Wade grumbled as he kicked off his shoes. He pulled off his shirt and shucked off his jeans. He stood there in his underwear, his hands awkwardly over his crotch.

"Jesus Wade, it's not like I haven't seen you naked before. Stop making such a production out of it."

"Yeah, it's just . . ."

"*Now* Wade."

He reluctantly pulled off his underwear. His semi-hard cock swung free, getting bigger as I looked at it. Wade glanced down at it and his face turned red.

"Good grief. Are you horny all the time, Wade?"

"It's the way you look at me, Kev," he grumbled. "You know it fucks with my head."

"Yeah, well that's not all I'm gonna be fucking. Now assume the position."

Wade bent over the kitchen table. I picked up his dog collar and buckled it around his neck.

"I should make you wear that to school," I growled into his ear. "So you don't forget your place."

Wade saw me pick up the paddle. He turned his head and looked back at me with big pleading eyes.

"Face forward, boy."

Wade slowly put his head down on the table. I waited for a few seconds, letting him think about what was coming. And then I let him have it.

The hardwood landed against his butt with a loud smack. It was followed by an even louder cry from Wade.

"Ow! God damn it! That hurts, Kev!"

"That's the idea. Now shut up and take your punishment like a man."

I hit him again. Wade clenched his teeth, trying not to make a sound. But it was no good. By the fifth strike, he was whimpering like a hurt dog. By the tenth, he was crying out in pain.

He sounded so pitiful that I almost felt sorry for him. I thought about cutting him a break and putting the paddle away. And then I remembered what it felt like, watching him laugh at me with all of his jock buddies, and calling me a faggot.

I laid into him, spanking him over and over again until my arm got tired. And then I switched the paddle to my left hand and started all over again. By the time I was done, Wade's ass was cherry red, and he was bawling like a baby.

"I'm sorry Kev!" he said, tears running down his face, "I am so sorry!"

He actually sounded like he meant it. And maybe he did, at that moment. But I knew Wade. At school the next day he'd be cozying up to his jock buddies again.

I put down the paddle and pulled the bottle of lube out of my pocket. Wade lay on the table sobbing, while I unzipped my jeans and oiled up my dick.

"Okay, boy. Time to show me how sorry you are."

I reached between his legs. Wade shuddered, as he felt the cold wet lube on his asshole. He lifted his head and looked back at me, his lower lip trembling. But I guess I didn't look like I was in a forgiving mood. Wade buried his face on the table again, readying himself for what was coming.

I ran my hand over his smooth butt, still red and hot from the spanking. And then I grabbed my dick and guided it up against his tight little asshole.

Wade let out a yelp, as I pushed hard and the head of my cock popped inside him. He banged his fist on the table, and his ass clamped down on my dick like a vise.

"Stop your whining, Wade. It's not like you're a virgin anymore. So shut up and take it."

I shoved another inch of my cock inside him, and Wade squealed like a stuck pig.

At first, I thought he was just being dramatic. But my dick is pretty big. And Wade had only been fucked once before. And even as mad as I was, I didn't want to actually rip him a new asshole. I pulled my cock back out.

"Come on Wade. You've done this before. Relax and take it."

Wade looked back at me and nodded.

I slid my dick back into him, more slowly this time. Wade clenched his teeth. But he forced himself to take it. Whimpering and squirming underneath me, as I fucked him with just the first two inches. And then the first three. Then four. Stretching his tight little ass out till he could handle the rest of my dick.

Wade moaned and gasped for breath, as it finally slid in up to the hilt.

"Good boy," I whispered in his ear.

I stood there for a few seconds. Grinding my hips against him slowly. Letting him get used to the feeling of having all nine inches of me inside him. And then I reached underneath him and grabbed his cock. He was rock-hard.

For the life of me, I can't decide if Wade loves being fucked or hates it. I'm not sure he knows, either.

I gave his cock one good pull. And that's all it took.

"Oh, fuck . . ." Wade muttered. "No!"

Wade's dick jumped to life in my hand and started shooting hot jizz all over the kitchen table.

I hadn't expected it to happen so fast. But if Wade was finished already, I was just getting started. I started plowing his ass hard and fast, determined to get my payback.

Wade moaned and grabbed the edges of the table, holding on for dear life while I gave him the fucking he deserved. Pounding his ass like a jackhammer. Over and over again, until we were both covered in sweat.

And then I finally cut loose. Wade let out a howl, as he felt my hot cum erupting inside him. He pushed himself up off the table, arching his back. And then somehow Wade was cumming. *Again*. Shooting another round all over the kitchen table. Jesus.

I held him tight against me while we both finished pumping our loads. It seemed to go on forever. And then Wade collapsed back onto the table, exhausted. I pulled my dick out of him, and fell back into a chair.

It took both of us a couple of minutes to catch our breath. Eventually, Wade stood up and turned around to face me. His beautiful jock body shining with sweat, his face all flushed. We just stared at each other for a while.

"So . . .um . . . are we done, Kev?" he finally asked.

"Yeah, we're done. Get out."

Wade picked his clothes up off the floor and slowly got dressed. As he was pulling on his varsity jacket, he looked at me sheepishly.

"Uh . . . Kev? For what's it worth . . . I really am sorry about today."

"Maybe," I said. "But not sorry enough to actually do anything about it."

* * *

THE COACH

Wednesday afternoon was a scorcher. Ninety degrees in the shade. The sort of day when no one wants to run around a field in football pads. Perfect for what I had in mind.

Right from the start of practice, I pushed the boys hard. Lots of speed and agility work. Blocking and tackling drills. Wind sprints. Half an hour in, they were all drenched in sweat and starting to grumble.

I was waiting for Wade to get fed up and mouth off to me. He didn't disappoint. I caught him sitting out one of the drills and talking to a girl in the bleachers.

"You too good for this, Johnson?"

Wade gave me his big old grin. The one that usually gets him out of trouble.

"Awe coach, I'll do the next one."

"Don't bother. Go ahead and take a break. There's the bench."

"Come on, Coach. You know what I meant. I'll . . ."

"No Johnson, I wouldn't want you to break a sweat with the rest of us mere mortals. So sit your delicate ass down on the bench. You can rest up while the rest of us practice."

"Coach . . ."

"*Now* Johnson."

Wade went and sat on the bench. He grinned at the other players and tried to laugh it off. But it was embarrassing.

And I was just getting started.

I wrapped up the drills and started the scrimmage. Wade stood up, ready to join in.

"Oh no, Johnson. I wouldn't want to interrupt your beauty sleep. You keep your ass on the bench. Danny, you'll be quarterback for this scrimmage. Run the flag plays."

Danny looked at me in surprise. He hesitated for a second, and then jumped to his feet.

"Yeah! Sure thing, Coach!"

The offensive players traded looks with each other. We had a tough game on Friday, and without Wade and his god-like throwing arm we'd be screwed. It was a weird time for me to be trying out a new quarterback.

I glanced back at Wade, sitting there awkwardly on the bench. I knew I'd have to put him back in sooner or later. But I wanted to take that arrogant bastard down a notch, first.

I heard the play start behind me. And then I turned around and saw Franklin running down the field with the ball, heading for a touchdown.

What the hell?

Defense must have made a mistake.

We set it up again, and I watched closely this time. It all started up like clockwork. Danny took the snap and dropped back with the ball. Tyler went deep. And then all of a sudden, out of nowhere, *Jeff Palmowski* had the ball. It happened so fast that I almost didn't see it. Neither did our defense. They were completely out of position, and Palmowski grabbed thirty yards before anyone managed to tackle him.

I called Danny over.

"What the hell was that?" I asked.

"It looked like a thirty-yard play to me, Coach."

"I told you to work on flag plays."

"If you want long bombs, put Wade back in," Danny said. And then he grinned. "But if you want to see our defense knocked on their asses, give me another ten minutes."

I looked him over. He was a cocky son of a bitch, and he was up to something. But I wanted to find out what.

"Okay, Danny. Show me what you've cooked up."

Danny took over the offense and called a series of plays. None of the standard ones that our team had been working on this season. And our defense had no idea what to do. They were all prepped to counter Wade's crazy long bombs. But Danny was throwing these short passes at lighting speed, and finding openings in our defense that I didn't even know were there. He didn't have Wade's power. But he was quick, and he was smart. And he was good at spotting an opportunity.

Something was going on. He hadn't been nearly this good last season. He must have done a lot of work over the summer. And from the look of it, he'd been practicing with a few of the running backs as well. Those plays weren't coming together out of thin air.

I left Danny in as quarterback for the rest of practice. He was still a little green. And once our defense wised up to his tricks things got more competitive. But he was definitely . . . interesting.

Plus, watching Wade stew on the bench was priceless. Just sitting there with nothing to do, while someone else played his position.

Yeah. You're gonna regret breaking our deal, Wade.

* * *

KEVIN

Wednesday night, I tried to get some homework done before Wade came over. I had an English paper and an economics project due, and I was dangerously behind on both. But I just couldn't make myself focus.

The problem is that even when I'm not fucking Wade, I'm still thinking about Wade. Stupid, random stuff that shouldn't matter. Like, the way that he came twice while I fucked him last night. Is that normal? Does he come twice when he's fucking his girlfriend? And why the hell should I care if he does?

And then there was that *stupid fucking kiss*. I knew it was idiotic to keep thinking about it. But I just couldn't get it out of my head. It was my first real kiss, so I realized that I was probably blowing it out of proportion. For Wade, it was like his hundred-thousandth kiss. He'd just done it from force of habit. He kisses girls when he cums, so he'd kissed me, too. Nothing more to it.

But still, I couldn't stop replaying the damn thing in my head. The look in his eyes right before he did it. His hand on the back of my neck. The feel of his tongue in my mouth.

Wade would probably be thrilled if he knew how much that one random kiss was fucking with my head. Payback for everything I've been putting him through.

He finally rang the bell a couple minutes after 8. I opened the door and let him in.

"You know the drill," I told him.

Wade nodded and started stripping down. I made him kneel while I buckled the dog collar around his neck. His obedience training seemed to be working, so I wasn't going to fuck with it now.

"Did you call me a faggot at school today?" I asked.

He looked at me and shook his head.

"No, Kev."

Well, not to my face, at least. I could only guess what kind of crap he'd said to his jock buddies behind my back. But I decided to give him a break from the paddle. It wouldn't seem like much of a punishment if he got it every night.

Instead, I sat down on the living room couch and ordered Wade to blow me. As soon as I unzipped my pants and pulled out my dick, Wade went right on it like . . . well, like a dog on a bone. He looked up at me, almost eagerly, noting my reaction to everything he tried. And every time he found something I liked, his eyes would light up and he'd really go at it.

I knew that he was just trying to get me off before I could fuck him. But it worked. I tried to hold back, but the feeling of Wade's mouth on my dick was too much.

"Oh . . . fuck," I muttered, as I grabbed his curly brown hair and shot my load into his mouth. Wade made a few muffled noises, but he took it.

When I was finally spent, he got up and walked into the kitchen. I heard him spit my cum into the sink. And then he came back and stood in front of me, his hard dick bobbing in the air between us.

"So . . . uh . . . Kev . . ."

"Yeah. We're done." I told him. "You can go."

"Uh . . . okay."

Wade picked up his underwear. I watched him getting dressed to leave, and then suddenly changed my mind.

"No. Don't go."

Wade paused in the middle of zipping up his jeans.

"What is it, Kev?"

That was the question. It's not like Wade and I had anything to talk about.

"I was wondering . . ." I started to ask, and then stopped.

"Yeah, Kev?"

"'Well . . .What's it like when you fuck your girlfriend?"

Wade looked at me funny.

"What?" I said. "I've never fucked a girl. I want to know."

Wade shrugged.

"It's . . . you know . . . pussy. It's good."

Well, that was articulate. I tried again.

"I mean, what's it like for *you*?"

"Well . . . it's . . . it's . . ."

He stammered on, trying to figure out how to explain it.

"Forget it," I finally said.

It had been a mistake to ask Wade to use words. It's not his strong suit. I'd have to find another way.

"Have you ever made a sex tape with your girlfriend?" I asked.

Wade grinned.

"Why? You want to watch, Kev?"

"Yeah."

That took him by surprise.

"But . . . you don't like girls. Do you, Kev?"

"No."

"Then why do you want to see me fuck one?"

I wasn't sure how to explain it. I didn't care about seeing his stupid girlfriend's tits or twat. I wanted to see what Wade was like with her. The way he kissed her. The look in his eyes when she made him cum. And whether or not the bitch could make him cum *twice*.

"I just do," I said.

Wade scratched his head, trying to figure me out.

"Well, you're out of luck, Kev. Brittany and I have never done anything like that."

"Then do it now," I ordered him.

Now Wade was really confused.

"I don't get it, Kev. Why?"

"Because I own your dick," I reminded him. "And if it's fucking someone I want to watch."

Wade looked at me like I was crazy. And maybe I was, a little. But he was my damn slave, so I was entitled to watch him fuck.

"And how am I supposed to get Brittany to go along with this?" Wade asked. "You think she's just gonna let me whip out my phone in the middle of sex and start filming her?"

"Yeah," I said. "That's exactly what I think."

Just like everybody else in this fucked-up town, I'm betting that she'll do anything Wade asks.

* * *

THE COACH

I opened Thursday practice with some hard physical training. And for once, Wade really threw himself into it. Pushing himself hard. Working up a sweat. With none of his sassy back talk for a change. After yesterday's humiliation, he was finally ready to buckle down and work.

We finished warm-ups, and I started the scrimmage.

"Tomorrow is our big game against the Wildcats!" I reminded everyone. "So show me what you've got!"

Wade ran onto the field with the rest of the team to take his usual position.

"Not you, Johnson!" I yelled at him. "Danny, I want you in as quarterback! Run some of the new plays we talked about."

Danny grinned and put on his helmet. Wade slowly limped back to the bench. He sat there, looking miserable, while Danny showed off his ground game. After a few minutes, Wade couldn't take it anymore.

"Come on, Coach. You can't just leave me on the bench!"

"You're right, Johnson. Get up and give me ten laps around the field."
"What?"
Wade looked at me in disbelief.
"You heard me, Johnson. Or are you too good to work up a sweat?"
Wade looked over at the scrimmage happening on the field. That had always been his place to shine. Having to watch from the sidelines was killing him.
"Well, boy?"
Wade looked at me, and then he reluctantly turned around and started running his laps. It had to be humiliating for him. Just running around the field, while everyone else practiced on it.

It took him almost twenty minutes to finish. Not bad, considering how much I'd worked him over at the start of practice. He came up to me after the last lap, drenched in sweat and panting for breath.
"That's all ten. Can I go in now, Coach?"
"Nah. Danny's working on a new play. Why don't you drop and give me fifty pushups."
"What? Are you crazy? I just . . ."
I gave Wade the look. He immediately backed down.
"No, it's okay, Coach. I'll do 'em."
He dropped to the grass and started counting them out quickly. Too quickly.
"Lower than that, Johnson," I said, putting my foot on his back. I pushed him down, till his chest was half an inch off the ground. "That's *one*."
Wade started his count over again.
"Okay Coach. One . . . two . . . three . . ."
"And give me a hand clap between each one."
Wade switched to the harder version. He was trying to power through them, but by twenty-five he was really struggling. I kept one eye on him while I ran the scrimmage with Danny.
"Forty-eight... Forty-nine . . . Fifty . . ."

I watched Wade slowly push out the last few. He hauled himself to his feet.

"Now can I go in coach?"

I ignored him.

"Nice play, Danny! Good job! Now try it with the fake."

Wade had to just stand there, while I ran more plays with Danny.

"Coach?" Wade finally said, meekly. "Coach?"

I looked over at him, as if I'd forgotten he was there.

"Oh yeah, Wade. Uh . . . why don't you do some wind sprints. You've been a little slow on your feet lately."

"But you said . . ."

"I said you need to do wind sprints, *boy*."

Wade looked like he wanted to punch me. But I could feel it. His submissive training was starting to kick in. He lowered his head.

"Yeah, coach. Anything you say."

"Okay. Here to the far bleachers. Fast as you can. And then jog back. Twenty times. Go!"

Wade took off.

I watched him run, and smiled to myself. This was going to be fun.

I kept working Wade like that all through practice. Inventing new tortures for him every time he asked to be put in. And then he realized that practice was over, and he'd never even gotten to hold the ball.

The other players all headed for the locker room, laughing and joking. Wade followed them, his head down.

"Not you, Johnson."

"But you said practice is over."

"It's over for them. You can give me another ten laps."

"But . . .but . . ."

Wade's face turned bright red. He wanted to fight me so badly. But he was beginning to understand that he had no choice but to obey. He slowly turned and headed back out to the field.

By the time I got to the locker room, the other boys had all hit the showers. I listened to some of their chatter. They thought it was kind of weird that I hadn't put Wade in at practice. But they figured that this was payback for all the backtalk that Wade has given me over the last couple of years.

And honestly? I think they all enjoyed seeing him taken down a peg.

By the time Wade finally came limping back into the locker room, the rest of the boys were leaving.

"Hey Wade! Great practice!" one of them yelled sarcastically.

Wade slowly shambled over to my office and knocked on the open door.

"Uh . . . coach? You got a minute?"

I looked up at him. He was drenched in sweat. Tired to the point of collapsing. Every muscle in his body aching. Just the way I wanted him.

"What is it, Wade?"

"So . . . I'm still gonna start tomorrow's game. Right?"

I leaned back in my desk chair and put my hands behind my head. I let him wait a good long time for my answer.

"I don't know, Wade," I finally told him. "I haven't decided yet."

"But . . . but . . . I did everything you told me to today! I ran the laps. I ran the sprints. I did *everything!*"

He looked like he wanted to cry.

"It's not fair!" he shouted. "I'm better than Danny! I'm the best quarterback you've got!"

I shrugged.

"Maybe. But you broke your word to me, Wade. And now I don't trust you."

I let the words sink in with him.

"Now get out of my office. I want to go home."

* * *

KEVIN

Thursday night, Wade turned up early.

"Jesus, Wade! I told you to be here at 8 pm, not 7:30! You almost ran into my mom leaving for work."

"Sorry, Kev."

I held the door open, and Wade limped inside. He was walking funny, like he'd somehow managed to pull every muscle in his body at the same time.

"What the hell happened to you?" I asked.

"Coach kind of kicked my ass at practice today."

Wade stumbled over to the couch and sat down.

"You sure you're okay?" I asked.

"Yeah, I'm fine," he said.

And then he gave me a sly grin, and pulled his phone out of his pocket.

"I managed to get that video you wanted."

"Already?"

"Yeah," Wade said, looking very pleased with himself. "I talked Brittany into sneaking out to the parking lot during lunch."

I sat down next to him. Wade put his arm around my shoulders, and then held up his phone so that we could watch. He pressed play.

I couldn't figure out what I was looking at. There was a lot of heavy breathing, and a couple of metallic circles moving up and down through frame. Eventually, I realized that I was looking at a couple of buttons on the front of Brittany's cheerleader uniform. Wade's camerawork left a lot to be desired.

Finally, the picture widened enough for me to get some context. They were in the back of Wade's car. Brittany was straddling him. From the way she was moving, she must have been bouncing up and down on his cock, but her miniskirt was concealing the actual penetration. Wade's bare shoulder was at the bottom of the frame. He must have been holding the phone up next to his head, trying to get a wide enough angle.

Then Brittany opened her eyes and saw what he was doing.

"Put that thing away!" she hissed at him.

"Awe c'mon," Wade said. "It will be fun."

"No way!" Brittany shouted, grabbing the phone and putting her hand over it. "I know you. You'll be showing this to all your stupid football buddies after practice."

"I'd never do that, babe. I *promise.* No one will ever see this but us. You're just so beautiful. I want you to see what you're like when we're together."

I don't think anybody can stay mad at Wade when he turns on the charm like that.

"Oh yeah?" she said.

"Yeah."

Brittany's hand slipped off the phone. She looked at Wade.

"You ever show this to anyone, and I'll rip your nuts off," she told him. "Got it?"

"Yeah babe, I know," Wade said laughing. He seemed to think that she was kidding. But she sure sounded serious to me.

And then she went back to riding his dick. The video caught every twinge of pleasure on her face as she humped away in the back of his car. But I couldn't see Wade's face. I couldn't see the way that he was looking at her. I had to settle for hearing him. And it sure sounded like he was enjoying it.

It only took her a couple of minutes to get Wade off. I heard him moaning, and then Brittany looked really pleased with herself as she felt his hot jizz shoot up inside her. I couldn't tell if she'd actually cum or not. She'd seemed to enjoy the whole thing, but there was never any big moment when she lost it. Maybe it's different for girls.

The phone panned down. Brittany lifted herself a little, and Wade's hard dick slipped out of her. It slapped down against his stomach, all slick and covered with cum.

"You like that, Wade?" Brittany's voice asked.

"Yeah babe, you're the best."

She leaned in to kiss him and the video stopped.

Wade put down the phone. He looked at me, grinning ear to ear.

"Pretty hot, huh Kev?"

"Uh . . . yeah," I mumbled.

I was frustrated. The video had cleared up a couple of mechanical questions I had about what Wade and his girlfriend did together. But it didn't tell me what I really wanted to know.

Wade sensed my disappointment.

"Isn't that what you wanted, Kev?"

"Yeah. That's what I asked you for," I agreed.

Wade put his phone away, looking a little hurt. Like some kid holding up a soccer trophy, and then being told that it was no big deal.

I had this sudden urge to bend Wade over the kitchen table and beat his ass with that wooden paddle again. I was angry, though I couldn't figure out why. I'd asked Wade to make the stupid video, and now I was mad at him for doing it.

Instead, I had Wade strip naked and lie down on the living room floor. And then somehow I wound up giving him a back rub. --He just looked so tired and pathetic that I couldn't help it. Some slave master I turned out to be.

Of course, I still fucked him afterward. Right there, spread eagle on the carpet. Wade tensed up as he felt the head of my cock pushing into him, and he realized that massage time was over. But I was getting better with practice, and I knew how fast Wade could handle my dick. He grunted a few times and balled up his fists. But he took it.

It was kind of fun, fucking Wade when he was too tired to put up a fight. I lay on top of him, pounding his ass, listening to his little whimpers.

His muscled jock body warm and sweaty underneath me. I wanted to fuck him like that for hours. But neither of us could hold out that long.

Wade gasped, as he felt my hot cum shooting up inside him. And then I felt all the muscles in his body tighten up, as he got ready to shoot his own load. I kept fucking him, even though I was done. Deliberately pushing him over the edge.

He pounded the floor with his fist, his body trembling. And then he let out this crazy yell and started shooting his load out all over the carpet.

"Good boy," I whispered in his ear.

When it was over, I lay on top of him for a while, catching my breath. And then I slowly pulled my dick out of him and sat down on the couch. Wade gingerly lifted himself off the carpet, and looked down at the sticky stain he'd made.

"Uh . . . Kev? You want me to clean that up?"

"Yeah. I guess you'd better."

Wade went to the kitchen and came back with paper towels.

"No, you need a damp sponge for that," I told him.

Wade looked at me blankly. Apparently, basic household chores are another thing that star quarterbacks are exempt from.

"Forget it. I'll do it."

Wade watched me clean up. And then he grabbed his clothes and started getting dressed.

"Did I say you can go?" I barked at him.

Wade looked at me, confused.

"But . . . we're done. Right, Kev?"

I looked at him, standing there with his jeans pulled halfway up. I didn't want him leaving just yet.

"You know what? I'm going to be horny again in an hour," I told him. "So you're not going anywhere. I'm gonna want to pound your ass again, slave boy."

"Uh . . . okay, Kev."

Wade shucked off his jeans and sat down in his underwear.

Of course, that left the question of what to do for the next hour while I waited for my dick to recharge. Well, I was behind on schoolwork. I got out my English book and went to work on my paper that was due.

Wade just sat there for a while.

"Uh . . . can I watch TV or something, Kev?"

"Sure."

I tossed him the remote. Wade started flipping through channels while I tried to focus on my paper. But then he started cheering.

"Oh man!" he yelled, "You didn't see that coming!"

I put down my book.

"What the hell are you watching?" I asked.

"The Ravager just sucker punched Captain Carnage while the ref wasn't looking, and now . . ."

Wade glanced over and saw the blank look on my face.

"You don't watch professional wrestling, Kev?"

"Why would I?"

"Seriously? Oh, you don't know what you're missing!"

Wade started explaining the finer points, while a bunch of characters jumped all over each other, threw themselves against the ropes, and beat each other over the head with folding chairs. The whole thing was completely idiotic, but before long I found myself cheering along with Wade and cursing the ref when he turned his back at the wrong moment. The show was sort of like Wade: so stupid that it was kind of fun.

And then Wade decided that he had to *show* me some of the moves. So he grabbed me and started pinning me down in various holds.

"This one is the backbreaker," he said proudly.

And then he flipped me around and put me in a headlock.

"And this one is the brainbuster."

I was laughing so hard that I couldn't tell him to stop. And then he pinned me down with my back on the floor.

"And this one is called the stripper."

He started pulling off my shirt. I grabbed his hands to stop him.

"Hey, what are you doing?" I asked.

"I'm taking off this stupid fucking T-shirt."

"Don't do that."

I struggled. But Wade was determined. And a hell of a lot stronger than I am.

"Come on, Kev. I'm naked here."

"That's because you're the sex slave."

"Yeah, well I'm a sex slave who can totally kick your ass."

He managed to peel my shirt off over my head. And then he sat down on my chest, pinning my arms to the floor with his knees. Looking down at me with this goofy grin.

"Get off of me, Wade."

I struggled, but he held me down easily.

"Seriously, Kev. Why do you always keep your shirt on when we fuck?"

I looked up at Wade. The muscles of his arms, his shoulders. And that chest. He was like some kind of Greek statue. And next to him I was just a skinny kid.

Wade saw the way that I was looking at him. He glanced down at his own chest, and then at mine. I saw a light go on behind his eyes, as it finally dawned on him.

"Do you not like the way you look, Kev?"

"Just get off me," I said, turning red.

Wade started laughing.

"Seriously dude? You can fuck me in the ass but you're worried that your chest isn't as big as mine?"

"Just shut up," I told him.

But Wade kept laughing.

"Kev, it's just… You've got nothing to worry about. I mean, you don't look like a football player. But you look . . . you know . . .like *you*."

"Well that's deep," I said sarcastically.

Wade rolled his eyes.

"I'm just saying, Kev . . . when you get to college, you're not going to have any problems. The other queer boys are going to be all over you."

"Yeah, right."

I'd seen enough gay porn and underwear ads to know the score. The gay world is going to be just like high school-- ruled by a bunch of muscle-bound jocks while the scrawny nerds stand on the sidelines.

Wade saw how red my face had gotten and stopped laughing.

"Okay, sorry. I didn't know this was a thing with you, Kev."

"Just get off me. Okay?"

Wade climbed off my chest and sat down on the floor next to me.

"You know Kev, if you're not happy with your body, I can take you to the gym. Show you how to use the weights."

"You'd do that?" I asked. "Seriously?"

"Sure. I'll be your trainer. Give me two months, I'll have you looking like Captain America. I'll kick your ass so hard in the gym that . . ."

"And what are the other football players gonna think when they see us hanging out together?" I asked.

Wade paused, and the smile faded from his face.

"Yeah. Right, Kev. I guess that wouldn't work."

"It's okay," I said.

I'd done the same thing. Wade and I have been spending so much time together that we keep forgetting that we're not actually friends.

We stopped talking and just sat there for a while, watching that stupid wrestling show. And then during the commercial break, I asked Wade why he hadn't gone out for the school's wrestling team.

"I can't," he said.

"Why not, if you like it so much?"

"My dad thinks wrestling is a fag sport," Wade said. "Plus, you know, I can't risk injuring *this*."

He held up his right arm.

"What's that got to do with it?"

Wade laughed, like he thought I was joking.

"Come on Kev. You've seen me throw a football."

"Actually no. I haven't been to a game."

Wade looked at me in shock. The idea seemed inconceivable to him.

"What? *Never?*"

I shrugged.

"Not my thing."

Wade stared at me, trying to wrap his mind around the idea.

"Jeez, Kev! You've never watched professional wrestling *and* you've never been to a football game? What the hell do you do for fun?"

"Homework and SAT prep. Some of us actually have to work to get into college."

"Bullshit," Wade said, punching me in the arm for no reason. "You're scary smart Kev. Colleges must be lining up to get a crack at that big bulging brain of yours."

"Sadly, no," I told him. "But you must be up to your neck in scholarship offers. Where are you gonna go?"

"I don't know. It depends on how I do this season. I'd like to stay close to home, so my Dad can come see me play. Maybe UT, if they make a good offer? Where do you want to go to college?"

"Any place that's not in Texas."

Wade laughed again, like he thought it was a joke.

"No," I said, "I'm serious. All I care about is getting out of this fucking state."

"Aw come on, Kev. You don't really mean that."

"Hell yes I do! You of all people should know how hard I have it around here."

Wade looked uncomfortable.

"Yeah," he mumbled, "I guess, but . . ."

"Remember how you and your friends tried to drown me in a toilet? And urinated into my locker?"

Wade's face turned a little red.

"Yeah, I guess I can see how that would piss you off, Kev"

"Damn right."

Wade turned back to the TV. He didn't say anything for a while.

"So . . . Kev? If you're not going to college in Texas, then I guess we won't see much of each other after graduation. Right?"

I looked at Wade. It was a weird question. Why the hell would Wade care where I went to school? And then I realized what was going on. Wade was worried that I'd follow him to college, keep blackmailing him, and fuck his brains out for the next four years.

"No," I reassured him. "Not much chance of that."

"Oh."

We sat there for a while, watching TV in silence.

"You know, Texas isn't all bad," Wade finally said. "There's some good stuff here."

"Yeah, if you're a straight jock, I'm sure it's great," I told him, getting fed up with the topic.

Wade turned to me, suddenly angry.

"You know what? Fuck you Kev!" he shouted. "My life isn't as fucking perfect as you think it is!"

I just stared at him.

"Where did that come from?" I asked.

Wade turned back to the TV.

"The crazy thing is . . . I don't even like football all that much," he mumbled.

"Okay, I'm calling bullshit on that."

"No, I mean it Kev. The game is kind of fun, and I like all the attention. But it's the *only* thing I've got. Ever since I was thirteen and my dad figured out that I could throw a football like nobody's business, it's been my whole fucking life. It's not like I picked football. It just sort of happened."

I fought back the urge to slap him.

"Wade, are you actually trying to get *me* to feel sorry for *you*? You've got the whole school eating out of your hand. Everybody wants to be your friend. You can fuck any girl you want to. And colleges are fighting each other to give you scholarships. You've got everything!"

"No, Kev. I've got *football*. And that's all I've got. I get tackled wrong and screw up my knee, or I tear a tendon in my shoulder, or . . . even if I just piss off my coach . . . and it can all be over. And the minute I'm no good for football, I'm no good for *anything*."

"Well, it still looks pretty good from where I'm sitting," I told him.

"That's cause you don't know what you've fucking got, Kevin!" Wade said, getting loud again.

"Yeah, I've got idiots like you pissing in my locker!" I yelled back.

"Okay . . . sure," Wade admitted. "But high school's almost over. And then you'll go away to Harvard or something and invent Facebook . . ."

"Mark Zuckerberg beat me to it," I corrected him.

"You know what I mean! You'll invent something *like* Facebook. And then you'll be rich and smart and all the queer boys out in California will be lining up to have you fuck them in the ass with that big dick of yours."

I looked at Wade, trying to figure out what the hell was going on in his head.

"Okay, why are we playing 'who's life sucks more?'," I asked. "And how the hell am I losing?"

Wade glared at me.

"Look in the fucking mirror sometime, Kev. You've got it better than you think you do."

Wade's face was all red. He was mad as hell, and for no good reason. I guess if you keep fucking a straight boy like a girl, he gets all moody and crazy like one, too.

"You know what?" I said. "I don't want to talk anymore. Let's fuck."

"Fine," Wade said. "What position would you like me in this time, *sir*?"

Wade put a nasty twist on the word *sir*. He might not know the meaning of "irony", but he had sure figured out "sarcasm".

"You know what? I want to fuck you the way you fucked your girlfriend."

I sat down on the couch, unzipped my pants, and pulled out my cock.

"Get down here and ride my dick, bitch."

"Of course, *sir*. Anything you say, *sir*."

Wade knelt down in front of me and started stroking my cock to get it hard. It only took him a few seconds. I can get a boner just from looking at Wade. Even when I am pissed at him.

Then Wade grabbed my jeans and started pulling them off.

"Don't do that," I told him.

I grabbed the belt loops to hold them up, but Wade slapped my hands away.

"If I'm going to be riding your dick wearing nothing but this fucking dog collar, then you can at least take off your stupid jeans, Kev."

He pulled my pants off, and then grabbed my boxers and pulled them off as well. I sat there wearing nothing but a pair of socks. Suddenly feeling very naked.

Wade climbed up on the couch and straddled me. His muscular legs on either side of mine. His chest just inches from my face. He reached down and grabbed my cock. He switched his grip a couple of times, trying to figure out how he was going to do this.

"It might work if you . . ."

"Shut up, Kev! I may not be a genius, but I can figure this out."

Wade shifted position again. He spit into his right hand. And then he lowered himself, guiding my cock into him.

"Oh . . . fuck," I moaned, as the head slipped inside him. Wade was still all warm and slick inside from the first load of cum that I'd shot into him. I felt my eyes roll back into my skull.

"You like that, Kev?"

I opened my eyes and saw Wade smirking down at me.

"Well, Kev?" he asked.

I just stared at him, not sure what game we were playing now. Wade lowered himself a little more, and another inch of my cock slid inside him. It felt so good that I started shaking.

And then Wade started grinding up and down. Fucking himself with just the first inch of my cock. The tease was unbearable.

"Okay! Yeah!" I gasped. "I fucking love it, Wade! Is that what you want to hear?"

Wade grinned.

"So maybe there's one good thing about Texas, Kev?"

Now I understood. I'd wounded Wade's competitive pride. If he had to take it up the ass, he at least wanted to know that he was good at it.

"Okay, fine," I agreed. "There's *one* good thing in Texas."

That seemed to make Wade happy. He took a few deep breaths, and then started lowering himself onto the rest of my cock. His own dick jumped to life and started to fill out. It flopped down on my stomach, semi-hard.

I saw him grimace.

"Does it hurt?" I asked.

"Not as much as the first time."

He clenched his teeth, but he kept at it. I watched, as inch after inch of my dick vanished into him. And then finally Wade was all the way down. His thighs resting on my legs, my cock inside him. He was breathing hard, and there was sweat dripping down his face. But he'd done it.

"You're getting good at this," I told him, stroking his thighs.

Wade shrugged.

"I like to be the best," he said, panting.

"It's a shame they don't give trophies for fucking," I told. "I'm sure you'd be all-state."

Wade punched me in the chest for that one. But he looked kind of pleased with himself all the same. And then he started riding me. Slowly grinding his ass up and down on my cock. I couldn't believe how good it felt.

I've always been in such a hurry every time we've fucked, that I've never had the chance to just sit back and watch him. The muscles of his legs, flexing against mine as he rode up and down on my dick. His abs rippling. His cock getting harder and harder until it was pointing straight up and slapping against his stomach.

Wade saw the way I was looking at him. He arched his back and flexed his arms.

"Now you're just showing off," I said.

Wade blushed a little.

He really did seem to get off on having me look at him. It's kind of crazy. You'd think that Wade could just glance at himself in the mirror and know how ridiculously hot he is. But it's like he can't feel it unless I'm staring at him.

We were both getting close. Wade started riding me faster. Sweat dripped down his chest and abs. His breathing got heavier. I saw him bite his lip. He had this weird expression on his face, like he was waiting for something. He looked down at me with those deep blue eyes.

And right then I knew. I just *knew* that this was not the way that he looked at his girlfriend.

I put my hand on the back of his hot sweaty neck and pulled his face down close to mine. I could feel him trembling. He looked back at me, a little scared.

And then all of a sudden our lips were locked and our tongues were wrapped around each other. I felt Wade moan into my mouth. And then he put his arms around me and pulled my body tight against his, as I shot my second load deep inside him, and his cum splashed over both our stomachs.

* * *

KEVIN

I woke the next morning with Wade curled up in my arms. His curly brown hair was tickling my nose, and sunshine was streaming in through my bedroom window. I lay there for a while, just enjoying the feeling of his warm skin against mine. For once, I didn't want to think. I didn't want to figure anything out. I just wanted to be.

And then I heard footsteps in the hallway. There was a knock on my bedroom door, and it started to open.

"Kevin! Time to get up for . . ."

"Mom!" I yelled. "Don't come in! I'm changing!"

That woke Wade up. He yawned and stretched.

"Quiet!" I whispered, "my mom's home!"

"You're running late today," she said through the door. "Try to hurry up."

"Yeah, mom. I'm on it."

Wade was snickering. I hit him in the arm to shut him up.

"Be quiet!" I told him. "Get dressed and . . ."

And then it hit me.

"Oh my God! Where are your clothes?"

I'd stripped Wade naked out in the living room. If mom saw his clothes lying out there . . .

"They're right here," Wade said, reaching down next to the bed.

He grabbed his underwear off the floor and pulled them on.

"I brought them in when I carried you to bed last night," he said.

Wade stood up and started pulling on his jeans. He seemed to think the whole thing was intensely funny.

"Relax, Kev. I've snuck out of a lot of girls' bedrooms. Never been caught once."

"Yeah, let's not make this a first."

I got up and locked my bedroom door. Wade kept laughing.

"I mean it!" I told him. "Be quiet!"

I wanted to slug the guy, but it's impossible to stay mad at Wade when he's smiling.

"You're gonna have to go out the window," I whispered.

Wade chuckled.

"At least your bedroom is on the ground floor," he said, pulling on his varsity jacket. "This one girl lived in an apartment on the sixth story. I had to . . ."

"Shut up!" I told him, opening the window.

He started to climb out.

"No, wait," I said.

There was one thing I needed to know. I grabbed him, pulled him close, and pressed my lips against his.

For a horrible moment, nothing happened.

And then Wade held my face in his hands and kissed me back. And suddenly everything was perfect. Maybe the only perfectly happy moment of my entire life.

And then the idiot started laughing again. I hit him in the arm.

"Okay, get out of here."

Wade got one leg out the window. But then he turned back to me, suddenly serious.

"Look, Kev . . . there's something I need to tell you about."

"Not now!"

"It's important," he insisted.

"NOT NOW! I'll meet you on the roof at school," I said, "Tell me then."

"Okay."

And then he just sat there in my window, grinning at me.

"So are you going?" I asked.

"Not till you give me another kiss."

I leaned in and kissed the idiot. Quickly this time.

"Now beat it, already!" I said, shooing him out the window.

Wade laughed and dropped to the grass. I watched him sneak around the back of our house, ducking so that he wouldn't be seen from the kitchen window, and then stealthily climb the fence. Yep, he'd had some practice at this.

I got ready for school. I still had a lot to figure out. But for the first time in my whole messed up life, it felt like everything might work out okay.

* * *

KEVIN

School on Friday was . . . weird. Tyler and Logan were still gunning for me. Apparently, they hadn't gotten the memo from the principal to back off. Or they just didn't care. So I was still playing "dodge the jock", hanging close to teachers so that the two of them couldn't beat me to a pulp.

At least Wade wasn't palling around with them. But that was only because he was spending every spare moment between classes making out with his girlfriend. I kept passing the two of them in the hall, swapping spit with each other. But when no one was looking, Wade would wink at me and smile.

I keep waiting for the moment when my life will start making sense. And then I wake up and remember that I'm in Texas. It's always going to be this fucking crazy.

I finally had a chance to meet Wade on the roof during fifth period. He looked around nervously as I climbed up.

"Did anyone see you?" he asked.

"No," I said. "We're alone."

"Good."

He took me in his big jock arms and planted a kiss on me.

"I've been waiting to do that all day," he said.

It might have been more convincing if his tongue hadn't been in his girlfriend's mouth for most of the morning. But it's hard to stay mad at Wade when he turns on the charm. He pulled me close, and our clothed bodies rubbed up against each other. I could feel his hard dick through the denim of his jeans.

"Jesus, are you *always* horny?" I asked.

Wade shrugged.

"Pretty much."

"So did you really want to talk? Or just make out?"

"Oh yeah," Wade said, suddenly getting serious.

"Look, Kev . . ." he said, and then stopped.

Wade has trouble finding words sometimes. I'm learning to be patient with that. I waited for him for to figure out how to say what he wanted to.

"We're friends now, aren't we Kev? All the bullshit aside. We are friends, right?"

He looked at me hopefully.

Honestly, I wasn't sure what to tell him. "Friendship" didn't seem like the right word to describe our relationship. I mean, he won't even talk to me in front of other people.

But then I looked into Wade's eyes. He wasn't asking for a discussion on semantics.

"Sure, Wade. We're friends."

Wade looked relieved.

"Good. Because I'm . . . well, I'm kind of in trouble with my coach."

I laughed.

"Wade, I don't know the first thing about football."

"Yeah. I know, Kev. But . . . well . . . see . . ."

"Do you want me to come to the game today?"

That seemed to catch him by surprise.

"What? Why would you do that, Kev? You hate football."

"Yeah," I agreed, "but I thought I might see what all the fuss is about. Find out why everyone is so in awe of that right arm of yours."

I thought that would make him happy. But Wade just seemed more upset.

"Should I not come to the game?" I asked. "I mean, nobody would know that I'm there because of you. I'd just sit in the stands and . . ."

"No! Kev, it's not about you! I did something . . . and now everything is all fucked up."

Wade was turning red. He really was freaked out about something. I put my arm around him.

"It's okay," I said. "Just tell me."

"It's . . . I . . . see... I . . ."

Wade stammered on for a few seconds, his face getting redder as he struggled to put it into words.

And then I heard a branch snap behind us. I turned around and saw the tree shaking, and heard voices. Someone was coming up for a smoke. And then two football players pulled themselves up onto the roof. They caught sight of Wade and me.

Fuck.

I turned back to ask Wade how he wanted to handle it. Just in time to see his fist flying at my face.

I don't even remember feeling the punch. But I remember Wade's voice.

"Get away from me you fucking faggot!"

I stumbled backward a few steps. Then I tripped and landed hard on my back, the wind knocked out of me.

"Woah! Wade just clobbered the queer!" a deep voice said.

And then other people were talking. A few faces were standing over me. But I was too out of it to react. I still couldn't believe he'd hit me.

"Let's fuck him up," someone said.

There was a clamoring of voices, and someone kicked me in the ribs. I curled up into a ball, trying to protect myself as the other jocks joined in.

"Guys!" Wade shouted, "He's learned his lesson. And you don't want to get suspended right before the game!"

There was some grumbling, and then they just left me there. I heard their big feet marching off across the roof, and some branches snapping as they climbed down the tree.

I lay there for a long time, trying to understand what had happened. Eventually, I sat up. My left eye hurt, and it was already swelling shut. I was gonna have one hell of a shiner. And my side ached where I'd been kicked. But it didn't feel like they'd broken anything.

I picked myself up and made my way to the nurse's office. He looked at me in shock.

"Jesus! What happened to you kid?"

I stared back at him.

"High school in Texas," I said. "That's what fucking happened."

* * *

THE COACH

The cheerleaders were whipping the crowd into a frenzy, but I was too tense to enjoy it. I'm always nervous before a close game.

At least I had the pleasure of watching Wade squirm. He'd lost all of his usual cocky bluster. Hell, today he looked downright depressed, like he'd lost his dog or his best friend in the world. Maybe he was finally starting to realize the consequences of being on my bad side.

He kept looking back into the stands, scanning the crowd like he was checking for someone in particular. Was he expecting a college scout or something? I hadn't heard about any coming. But maybe Wade knew something that I didn't.

The cheerleaders wrapped up their show, and the Wildcats' defense took the field. They're a tough team. Strong fast players. Smart coach. We hadn't won a game against them in three years. And in Texas, we have a special word for football coaches who don't win games.

Unemployed.

I took another look at Danny, sizing him up. He looked more like a gymnast than a quarterback. Short, and blond. If cuteness could win football games he'd be perfect.

And then I looked at Wade. My prize fucking stallion. I'd been grooming him for two years, honing that arm of his into a laser accurate weapon. Wade was the safe play. The smart play. But putting him in would mean backing down. I'd have to admit that I needed that arrogant bastard to win. And then he'd fucking *own me.* I'd never break him.

"Well coach?" asked Logan, one of my wide receivers.

I took a last look at my two options.

"Danny, you're starting. Everybody hit the field."

Wade looked at me in disbelief.

"But coach . . ."

"You made your fucking bed, Wade. Now lie in it."

As Wade sat down on the bench, I could hear the muttering behind me in the stands. The fans wondering what the hell was going on. Wade was probably the best quarterback in the league. And here I was starting tiny little Danny Sherman. They had to think I was crazy.

Maybe I was.

Danny called the first play. The center snapped the ball to him. Danny dropped back. And then…

And then *it was beautiful!* The Wildcats' defense had no idea what happened. They'd been prepped for Wade and his crazy long bombs. Instead, Danny pump-faked left and then nailed a short pass to an unguarded running back on the right. The Wildcats were literally tripping over each other as they tried to figure out what had happened.

It turned out to be the best game of my life. Our defense held its own, and even managed to snag an interception in the second quarter. But on offense… Danny just made monkeys out of the Wildcats. Their coach was frantically calling time-outs, trying to switch up their defense on the fly. But he just couldn't do it fast enough. After our third touchdown, the fans stopped asking about Wade, and were cheering Danny like he was the second coming.

And the best thing of all was watching Wade. Sulking as he sat on the bench. Watching the team win without him. Realizing that he's not as indispensable as he thought. Not so cocky now, are you?

It was supposed to be a close game, but it turned into a massacre. So with five minutes left, I decided to twist the knife. I sent Wade in for our final possession, along with most of our second-string offense. Making it obvious that I was only putting him in because we were so far ahead.

I almost felt sorry for him. The Wildcats' defense may have been frustrated by Danny, but they knew *exactly* what to do with Wade. They were prepped and ready for his game, and they shut him down mercilessly. He kept trying to fire off one of his bombs, but our second stringers just couldn't get open for one.

And then, with ninety seconds left in the game, it happened. Wade took the snap and dropped back, desperately trying to find an opening. Any opening. But the Wildcats' defense was all over our wide receivers. And our second-string blockers didn't protect Wade the way they should have. --Hell, they're only juniors.-- Three defenders got through and sacked Wade, knocking him backward.

And he *fumbled!* Golden boy Wade dropped the ball! One of the Wildcats dove on it, transferring possession to their team. I almost wanted to cheer.

Wade pounded the ground with his fist, and then slowly got up and walked off the field. The Wildcats' offense came out to take possession, but it didn't matter. We were way ahead on the scoreboard, and they didn't have time to go for a touchdown. In the end, they were able to grab a field goal, but it didn't affect the outcome.

As the buzzer announced the end of game, our fans went wild. The team dumped a cooler of ice over Danny. And then they picked him up and carried him back to the locker room, cheering.

Wade slowly trailed behind them, walking alone.

The principal came up and congratulated me on the game, along with a bunch of parents. And then Wade's dad cornered me.

"What the hell is wrong with you!" he growled. "Why did you keep my boy out of the game like that?"

I shook my head, as if I was sorry to deliver the bad news.

"Look Frank, your boy's got a lot of talent. But he's also got a lot of mouth and a lot of attitude. And the fact is, he's lazy. He's just not living up to his potential."

Wade's dad was stunned. For the last few years, all he's ever heard is how proud he should be of his son, and what a great future Wade has. Frank turned and walked away quickly.

I saw him catch up to Wade, and grab him by the arm. While I stood there accepting congratulations, Wade's dad started yelling at him, right in front of everybody.

"What the fuck is this I hear about you mouthing off to your coach? And how the HELL did that fumble happen?!"

I tried not to smile, as I headed back to the locker room.

The boys were tired but in high spirits. Danny was the man of the hour. The rest of the team was all laughing and joking with him in the shower.

Acting like they'd always been best buddies. I guess they'd forgotten about him fucking their girlfriends.

Wade finally limped in just as the last of the other boys were leaving. That tongue-lashing from his father must have gone on for a while. He walked through the empty locker room, his cleats loud on the cement floor. He knocked on the door of my office.

"Coach?"

I looked up at him, standing there in his uniform. Looking like he was about to cry.

"Yeah, Wade?"

"I was just wondering… Is this the way it's gonna be from now on?"

I shrugged.

"We won, didn't we?"

"Yeah," Wade said. "But . . . you know . . . maybe you could start me next game?"

"And why would I do that?" I asked.

"Because I'm good! I'm really good at this, right?"

I shrugged. Wade's lower lip started to tremble.

"I'll try harder, coach! I'll do better! I promise!"

"Your promises don't mean a lot anymore, Wade."

I could see the tears welling up in his eyes.

"But Coach . . . football is all I've got. I don't have *anything* else."

"You should have thought of that before you broke your word."

Wade just stood there in the doorway. I pretended to read through some papers on my desk. Letting him think about it.

"Coach? Is there anything I could . . . maybe do?"

I didn't even look up.

"I'm done bargaining with you Wade. I need boys who are willing to give me 100%. No limits. Since you can't do that, I've got no use for you."

Wade blinked back his tears. He stepped into my office and closed the door behind him.

I didn't say anything. But I pushed my chair back from my desk.

Wade swallowed hard, and then walked over and knelt down in front of me. He reached for my belt buckle with trembling hands. I watched him unzip my pants and pull out my cock. He stared at it for a few seconds, trying to decide if he was really going to do this. And then he wrapped his lips around it.

The warm wet feeling of his mouth on my dick was nothing compared to the feeling of *winning*. Of beating that cocky bastard and showing him who was on top.

Wade looked up at me, my dick in his mouth.

"Am I supposed to be impressed?" I asked.

Wade lowered his gaze and went to work. Licking and sucking, his face bobbing up and down on my cock.

And he was *terrible*. I mean truly, seriously, awful. It was like he'd never blown a guy in his life.

"What the hell are you doing?" I asked.

Wade looked up at me confused.

I don't understand Wade. I'd caught him wearing that crazy dick restraint, so I know that he's some S&M master's trained bitch. But he keeps trying to pull this "poor little innocent schoolboy" bullshit with me, acting like he's never given a blowjob or taken it up the ass. And I was running out of patience with him.

I grabbed him by the hair and shoved the rest of my dick in his mouth.

"I know you've deep-throated before, so quit stalling!"

I felt the head of my dick slamming against the back of his mouth. Wade started gagging and coughing, still trying to act like he had no idea how to do what I was asking.

I face fucked him hard a few more times, banging away until I finally felt my dick sliding down his throat.

"There you go."

Wade gagged and made some more choking sounds, but I kept sliding my meat down his throat until he'd swallowed the whole thing.

"That's the way you take it," I told him.

Wade looked up at me, his lips wrapped tight around the base of my cock, his blue eyes filled with tears. Maybe from gagging on my dick. Or maybe because he finally understood his position. Whoever's bitch he'd been before this, he was mine now.

I let go of his hair, and let him try again. I watched him go at it, my cock vanishing into his mouth. His oral skills were pathetic, but it didn't matter. I had time to train him. And today, I could get off just from knowing that I *owned* him.

I felt myself getting close. I grabbed the back of Wade's head and held him down while I shot my load into his sweet little mouth. Wade made some muffled cries of protest, but I was having too much fun to care.

When I was done, I leaned back in my chair. Wade looked away from me, and then spat on the floor.

"What the hell was that?" I asked him.

I slapped him hard across the face. Wade looked at me, terrified. Like he had no idea what he'd just done.

"Did I tell you to spit, boy? Next time I give you my cum, you will swallow every precious drop! And count yourself lucky to be carrying my jizz inside you."

Wade grimaced, like he couldn't stand the idea. What the hell had his first master been teaching him? The boy was going to need some serious work.

Wade got up and started walking to the door.

"Where the hell are you going?" I asked. "Did I say we were done?"

"Uh . . . no sir."

I got out my phone and held it up to record video.

"Take off your uniform, boy."

Wade looked at the phone.

"What are you doing, Coach?"

"I want a little something to take home with me. So strip out of your uniform."

Wade reached out to put his hand over the phone, but I pulled it back.

"Look Coach, I'll do anything you want. *Anything*. But don't make me do it on camera."

I shook my head.

"Here's the thing, Wade: You've already broken your word to me once. So I want some insurance. Something I can hold over your head to make sure you behave for the rest of the season."

"But Coach . . ."

"Do you want to play football or not? It's either this, or your ride the bench all season. And then good luck convincing those college scouts to give you a scholarship."

Wade thought about it longer than I expected him to. I could almost see him breaking inside.

"You won't show it to anyone else?" he asked, a little desperately.

"Not if you keep your promise," I reassured him. "If you do *everything* I want, I'll delete it at the end of the season."

Wade bit his lip. And then he slowly pulled his jersey off over his head.

"That's it."

I filmed him in loving detail as he stripped down. Taking off his shoulder pads. His cleats. Revealing more and more of his hot nineteen-year-old body. By the time he was down to his jockstrap, Wade's face was burning red.

"Come on, Wade. I haven't got all day."

Wade turned away from the camera and took off his jockstrap. I got a nice shot of his perky little butt. And then he just stood there, too ashamed to turn around.

"No point in being shy now Wade. Show us your dick."

Wade slowly turned to face me. No wonder his face was so red. The boy had a raging boner. For all the fuss he makes about it, he likes being used and treated like meat.

"Are we done now, coach?" he asked in a small voice.

"Not yet. You're gonna jack off for the camera."

"But coach . . ."

"Now, boy."

Wade looked down at his rock-hard cock, humiliated. He reluctantly grabbed it and started pumping. I remembered that the boy has a hair-trigger dick, so I knew that I didn't have long. I got a good shot of him working his cock, and then I panned up his body. When I got to his face he tried to look away.

"Face the camera, boy."

Wade turned back and looked into the lens. And then I saw the look in his eye.

I heard him give a little whimper, and I pulled back just in time to catch the money shot. Wade leaning back against my desk, pumping his dick as his hot cum splashed all over his stomach. Hell, I think some of it ended up in his hair. The boy really does shoot an impressive load.

When he was done, he looked back at me.

"Are we done now, sir?"

"Almost," I said.

I ran my free hand over his stomach, scooping up a handful of his cum. I held it up to show the camera. And then I shoved it into Wade's mouth.

Wade let out a surprised gurgle and made a disgusted face. He tried to spit it out, but I clamped my hand over his mouth.

"Now swallow, bitch. For the camera."

A tear rolled down Wade's cheek. He took a second to prepare himself for it. And then he made a pained face as he swallowed his first load. And the camera captured every delicious moment of it.

"Good boy," I said, "Open your mouth."

Wade did as he was told. I shot a close-up of his mouth, just to prove that he'd swallowed. And then I finally switched off my phone.

I kissed Wade roughly, enjoying the lingering taste of cum in his mouth. He pulled away after a couple seconds, but I let it go.

"Next time I shoot in your mouth, you're gonna swallow every drop. Right boy?"

Wade nodded slowly. He was beaten. He wasn't broken, yet. That would take time and work. But he was beaten, and he knew it.

"Yes, sir."

"Okay," I said, slapping him on the ass. "Hit the showers."

Wade headed for the door to my office.

"And Wade?"

He turned back to me.

"Yes, sir?"

"One last thing: Who owns your ass?"

He didn't even hesitate this time.

"You do, Coach. You own my ass."

Did you enjoy this book? Then help other readers discover it! Take a moment to review it on Amazon.

And Check out the continuing action in . . .

Settling The Score-- Season 2: Breaking Point

Coach Davis should be happy. His team is on a winning streak. And his arrogant star quarterback, Wade Johnson, has finally learned to shut up and do what he's told. It turns out that all Wade needed was a firm hand . . . and the threat of blackmail.

Now the coach has Wade in a special kind of training. Pushing him past all his limits. Wearing down his resistance. Teaching him the meaning of unconditional obedience. Properly broken and conditioned, Wade is going to be one hell of a player. And an even better fuck slave.

There's just one problem-- Wade is holding on to a secret. Someone else had already given the cocky straight boy a taste for being fucked and dominated. And no matter what the coach threatens, Wade won't give up the guy's name.

The coach doesn't like to share. So he's going to find out who Wade is protecting. Wade's got to learn that he has no one to turn to. No one to trust. No one who's going to ride to his rescue. Wade's got to learn that he belongs to the coach.

And no one else.

Looking for other Josh Hunter series to read? Check out . . .

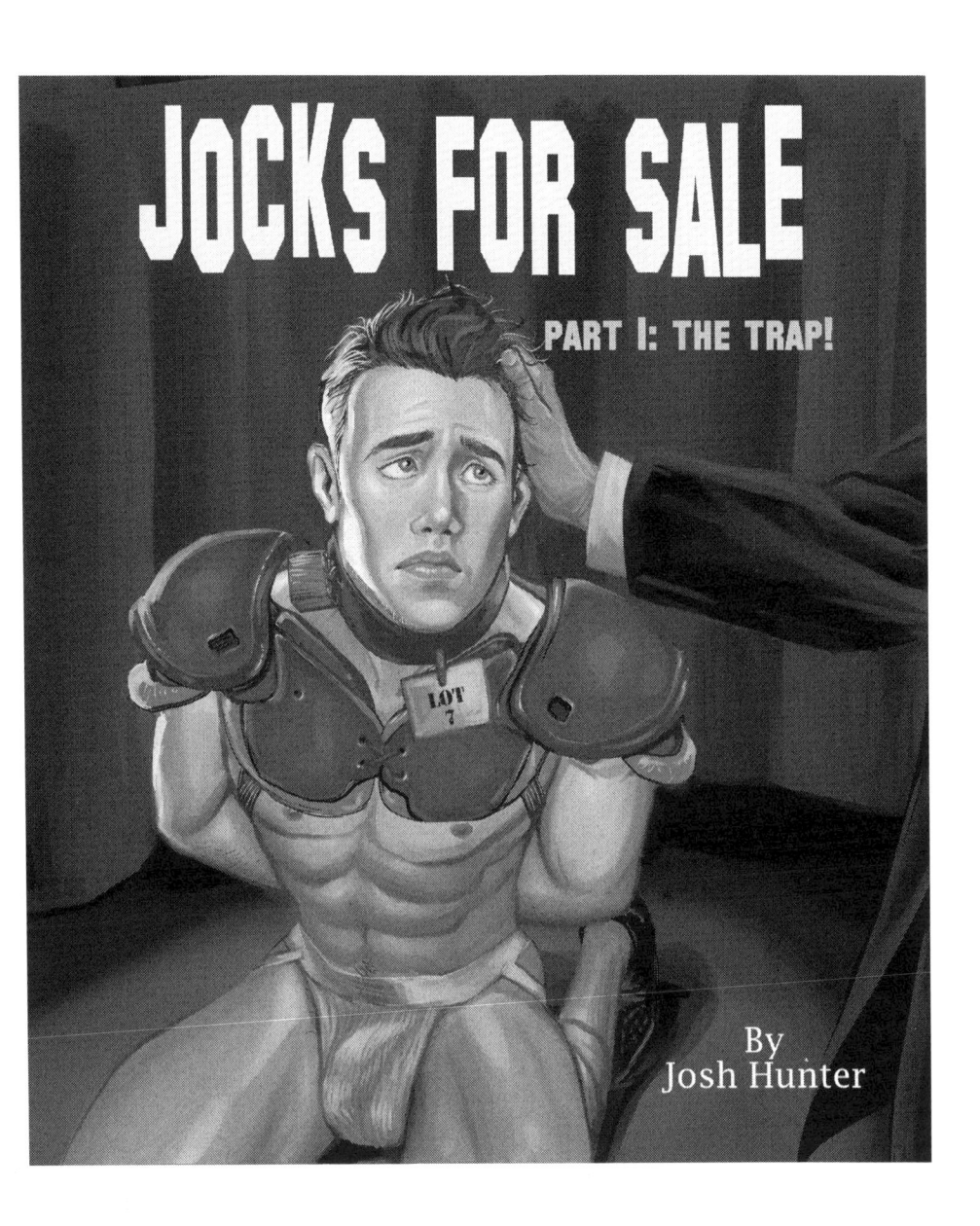

These fraternity boys just made a BIG mistake.

Spring break in Cancun was supposed to be a non-stop party. Beer, sun, and bragging about all the hot girls that they'd hooked up with. Getting kidnapped by a criminal syndicate was not part of the plan.

Now these golden boy athletes have fallen into a shadowy world they never knew existed. A world where rich men collect boys like them for fun. A world where they will be broken, trained, and sold to the highest bidder.

Can the cocky jocks find a way to fight back and escape? Or is it already too late?

Read it now on Amazon!

Want to keep up with all of Josh's stories?

Sign up for his dark erotic newsletter at JoshHunterXXX.com

Made in the USA
Columbia, SC
10 April 2025